What Was That?

It sounded like whispering. A voice. Nearby. No. It couldn't be. It was the wind.

Again she heard it. She shivered from the cold, from surprise, from sudden fear. She gripped the wheel of the car tighter still and stared straight ahead.

What was it saying? She could hear it so clearly. A whisper right in her ear. Did it say her name?

Yes. That's what it sounded like.

Melissssssssssa. Just wind. Cold wind in her ear. Cold wind whispering so softly in her ear.

Melissssssssssa . . .

Her friend's house was just a few blocks away. I can make it, she thought, staring straight ahead, ignoring the whispering wind that repeated her name so insistently, so menacingly.

I can make it. If I can just keep control of the car . . .

"No!" she cried out, as something—or someone—seemed to grab the wheel!

Books by R. L. Stine

Available from ARCHWAY Paperbacks

FEAR STREET
R·L·STINE

Haunted

AN ARCHWAY PAPERBACK
Published by POCKET BOOKS
New York   London   Toronto   Sydney   Tokyo   Singapore

AN ARCHWAY PAPERBACK *Original*

An Archway Paperback published by
POCKET BOOKS, a division of Simon & Schuster Inc.
1230 Avenue of the Americas, New York, NY 10020

ISBN: 0-671-74651-0

First Archway Paperback printing July 1990

15 14 13 12 11 10

Fear Street is a trademark of Parachute Press, Inc.

AN ARCHWAY PAPERBACK and colophon are
registered trademarks of Simon & Schuster Inc.

Printed in the U.S.A.

IL 6+

Haunted

chapter

1

Melissa Dryden sat up in bed and screamed.

Still half asleep, she felt the fear fall over her like a suffocating blanket.

She screamed again as the noise at the bedroom window grew louder. "No—please! Don't come in here!"

She started to scramble out of bed, but her legs were tangled in the bed sheet. Breathing hard, trying to choke back her panic, she tugged herself free and stumbled toward the door—just as her father burst in.

"Lissa—what is it?"

She ran to him, ran behind him for protection, and pointed to the window. "Someone is out there," she managed to say.

The noise at the window grew louder.

1

"Huh?" He squinted toward the window. He must not have had time to find his glasses in the dark. He heard the noise. He shook his head as if trying to wake himself up, then pulled the belt on his flannel bathrobe tighter.

Melissa tried to stop him, but he plunged ahead toward the window. "No, Dad, wait—" He was always so reckless. Didn't he ever stop to think about the danger?

Melissa backed up and bumped into her bed table. "Ow!" Her phone crashed to the floor. The noise startled her.

She wanted to run, run from the room, run from the house. But she couldn't leave her dad.

Why was he laughing?

"Come here, Lissa."

"What?" She tugged at her tangles of blond hair with both hands.

"I said come here."

"What is it?" She took a few hesitant steps toward the window.

Mr. Dryden, smiling and shaking his head, held back the curtain with one hand and pointed outside with the other. "Here's your prowler."

Melissa heard the tapping noise again. A loud tapping followed by a scraping sound. Still halfway across the room, she didn't go any closer. "It's a tree branch, right?"

"Right."

"What on earth!" Melissa's mother came scurrying

2

·into the room and flicked on the lamp. "What's going on?"

"Nothing to be concerned about," Mr. Dryden said, looking out at the sky. "Full moon. Look at that. The moon's always so big in August."

"I don't want to hear about the moon. I want to know what all the screaming was about," Mrs. Dryden said sharply.

Mr. Dryden let the curtain fall back into place. He tugged at his bathrobe belt. "Lissa heard a tree tapping at her window."

"A tree?"

Melissa sighed loudly. "I thought it was a burglar," she said, plopping down on the bed. "I was asleep and I guess the noise woke me up and—"

"You shouldn't watch the news before you go to bed," Mrs. Dryden said. She walked over and squeezed Melissa's hand. "All the talk about that prowler—"

"Well, there *is* a Fear Street Prowler, Mother," Melissa said, her voice rising several octaves. "I didn't imagine *that*, you know. Someone *has* been breaking into houses on Fear Street and—"

"We've lived on Fear Street for five years," her mother said, pushing Melissa's thick hair back off her forehead. "We've never had the slightest problem. Don't you ever brush your hair?"

"I like it wild."

"Hey—what are you wearing, Skinnybone?" Her father walked over, staring at her nightshirt.

"Don't call me Skinnybone. You promised," Melissa whined.

"You know she's sensitive about that," Mrs. Dryden scolded her husband. "Why do you insist—"

"What are you wearing?" Mr. Dryden demanded, pulling on Melissa's sleeve.

"Oh. Uh . . . it's one of your old pajama shirts, I think."

"I've been looking all over for that," her father yelled, looking up at the ceiling. He was always complaining straight to the heavens. "I spent hours searching my dresser and—"

"Sorry. I thought it was old."

"Of *course* it's old. That's why I like to wear it. Why can't you wear your own clothes? I don't wear *your* clothes, do I?"

Melissa laughed. Her father weighed two hundred pounds, more than twice as much as she did. "You're welcome to, Dad. Anytime."

Mrs. Dryden glanced at the clock radio on the bed table and frowned. "Why are we exchanging clothes at three-thirty in the morning?"

"Sorry, Mom," Melissa said. She slid under the sheet. "I'm okay. We can go back to bed now."

"What time did you get in tonight?" Mrs. Dryden asked. "Late, I'll bet."

"Yeah. It was pretty late. I'm not sure when."

"Pretty late or very late?"

"Come on, Mom," Melissa said impatiently, sitting up. "Summer's over in a week. Buddy and I haven't

4

had a chance to see each other. He was away on vacation with his parents for two weeks and—"

"Well, that's why you're screaming your head off, imagining prowlers. You're overtired."

Melissa groaned. Her mother's explanation for *anything* that ever happened was "You're overtired." If you messed up on a test, or didn't feel like eating, or were in a bad mood, it had to be because you were overtired.

"Mother, for the last time, there really is a prowler on Fear Street. I didn't imagine that. It's in the newspaper practically every day."

"It's so hot in here," her mother said. She never could stick to a subject. Her mind flitted from one thing to another like a bee buzzing from flower to flower. "It's eighty degrees outside. Why don't you open that window?"

"I—I really don't want to," Melissa said, feeling a little of the fear creep back.

"Well then, let's go to bed. Are you coming, Wes?" She pulled her husband's sleeve.

"Yeah. Sure. But come here a minute, Lissa. I want to show you something."

"Huh? Can't it wait till morning?" Melissa suddenly felt very sleepy.

"No. Come on." He grabbed both of her hands and pulled her easily out of bed. "Wow, you're so light."

"Are you starting in again about how skinny I am?"

"No. Come on. I want to show you something that will make you feel better."

5

His expression grew serious as he pulled her across the hall to their bedroom.

"Wes, really—let her get some sleep. She's very overtired," her mother said, following behind.

"This'll only take a second. I want to calm her down," Mr. Dryden said, clicking on the ceiling light.

They stepped into the large bedroom, all shades of blue, which always smelled of Mrs. Dryden's perfume. Melissa's father pulled her to his bed table and then let go of her hands.

He pulled the drawer of the bed table out nearly as far as it would go and reached into the back of the drawer. "Here it is," he said, a grim smile on his round face.

He held up a small silver pistol.

Melissa's mouth dropped open in surprise. "A gun? Is it real?"

Mr. Dryden dropped it into her hand. It felt much heavier than it looked and was cold to the touch. "Of course it's real. And it's loaded."

Melissa shuddered and quickly handed the gun back to him.

"Hey, don't look so terrified." He spun the gun around on his finger. "You know, I've been hunting since I was ten. I know a thing or two about guns."

"Put it away, Wes," Mrs. Dryden said from the other side of the bed. She yawned loudly.

"I bought it right after I read the first news story about the Fear Street Prowler. I just wanted to show Lissa that if he ever does try to break in here, I'll be ready for him."

6

"Thanks, Daddy," Melissa said, pushing a tangle of hair off her face. Normally she would have made a joke or said something sarcastic, but she was just too tired.

"The gun is always here in this drawer," Mr. Dryden said, carefully replacing it and sliding the drawer shut.

"Good night," Melissa said.

"Good night." Her mother was already under the covers.

"I want that shirt back tomorrow," Mr. Dryden called after her.

Melissa crept back to her room, turned off the lamp, and climbed into bed. The tree branch was still tapping gently against the windowpane. She pulled the covers up over her head and tried to ignore it.

She turned onto her back, then after a few minutes slid onto her side. Despite her weariness, she couldn't fall asleep. What a terrible night! First the argument with Buddy. Then the false alarm about the prowler.

She thought about Buddy. She had been so glad to see him. It had been two whole weeks, after all. He looked so tan, so handsome after two weeks at the beach.

They had so much to talk about. So she hadn't minded when he suggested they borrow his dad's car and drive up to River Ridge to talk. River Ridge, high above the Conon. . . ka River, was one of the prettiest spots in Shadyside. It was also the favorite makeout spot of kids from Shadyside High.

Buddy drove really fast. Melissa had to plead with

him to slow down. He pulled into a secluded spot overlooking the river and cut the engine and lights.

"So tell me about your vacation. Did you meet any cute girls?" Melissa teased.

Instead of replying, Buddy had pulled her close and wrapped his arms around her. They kissed, a long, lingering kiss.

"Buddy, I thought we came up here to talk. I haven't seen you for weeks."

He pushed her hair back behind her shoulders with both hands. "We can talk later."

"No, Buddy—"

But he didn't want to take no for an answer.

Before Melissa even realized it, he had slipped a hand under her blouse.

"Move your hand!" She pulled away from him. "Come on, Buddy!" She reached for the door handle.

He looked very surprised. "Hey—what are you doing? I thought you'd be glad to see me."

"I *said* I wanted to talk."

He apologized, and then apologized some more. But as far as she was concerned, the evening was ruined. What was the matter with him, anyway? He had never acted like that before.

"Let's start over," he suggested, looking very unhappy. They tried to have a normal conversation then, but it just didn't work. Melissa still felt surprised and angry, and Buddy was obviously angry too. A short while later they drove home in silence.

As Buddy pulled up the drive, he apologized again. He really sounded as if he were sorry. She kissed him quickly on the cheek and ran into the house, more upset with herself than with him.

Now as she turned over in bed, trying to get comfortable, feeling very hot, her hair wet and matted against the back of her neck, she blamed herself for spoiling their reunion date. Maybe she had overreacted. Sure, he came on too strong a lot of the time. Sure, he could be pushy, even selfish at times. But he really did care about her. And most of the time he was a great guy.

If only she could stop thinking and get to sleep. It must be after four in the morning.

She punched the pillow, fluffing it up. The tree limb tapped against the window, three short taps. She pictured her father removing the pistol from the bed-table drawer with that grim smile.

The silver pistol. She saw him spin it on his finger.

"The gun is always here in this drawer," he had said.

Despite the heat of the room, Melissa shuddered.

There was something so frightening about that little silver pistol, lying there in the drawer, just waiting to be used.

chapter

2

*M*aybe I should tie my hair back, Melissa thought. Lying on her stomach on her bed, trying to read a book, she pulled at her hair with her free hand and kept pushing strands out of her face.

"Why don't you get it cut before school starts?" her best friend, Della O'Connor, had asked a few days earlier. Della had perfect hair—straight, black, and long, past her shoulders, and it always fell perfectly into place.

"I like it wild like this," Melissa had replied. After all, what good was hair if you couldn't toss it, pull it, play with it, and swing it around? Melissa didn't want perfect hair—she wanted hair with personality!

If only it would stay out of her eyes while she read.

"And why am I reading this Stephen King novel?" she asked herself. "There I was, scared silly by a twig on the window last night, and this afternoon I'm reading this creepy book."

She read a little longer, then looked up.

The room suddenly felt cold.

Had she imagined it?

No. The air was cold, as if a wintry breeze had blown in.

She looked at the window. The afternoon sun was still high in the sky. The curtains weren't blowing. There was no breeze at all.

Still cold, she closed the book and stood up. Shadows from the trees outside her window played against the wall. She heard the front door slam downstairs.

"I'm home!" her father yelled.

He's home early, she thought. What's going on?

"Lissa—are you home?" He was calling from the foot of the stairs.

"Yes, I'm here, Daddy." Forgetting about the strange chill in the room, she tossed the book on her bed and hurried down the stairs. The air felt warm as soon as she left her room.

Mr. Dryden, his eyeglasses sliding down his nose as usual, watched her descend the stairs with a strange smile on his face.

"What's that smile for, Daddy? Aren't you home a little early?"

He put on a phony hurt expression. "Aren't you glad to see me?"

"No. Not at all," she replied with a straight face.

"Well, I think you'll be glad when you see what I have for you. Where's your mother?"

"She flew to Florida. She wants to surprise you with a tan at dinner. What do you have for me?"

"No. Really. Where is she?"

"At the mall. Where else?"

He looked disappointed. "Oh, well. I can't wait for her. I have to show you." He remained where he was and slowly pushed his glasses up. They slid right back down his nose.

"Show me what? Come on! Are you deliberately keeping me in suspense?"

He laughed. "Maybe I am. Maybe I should make you guess what your birthday surprise is."

"Birthday surprise? But my birthday isn't until Friday." She frantically tried to think of what he could have bought her. He hadn't even asked what she wanted.

What did she want? She couldn't think of anything. A new Walkman, maybe. Some CDs . . .

"Maybe I'll make you wait till Friday," he said, obviously teasing. "Let's change the subject." He loosened his tie and started to remove his suit jacket.

"No way!" Melissa cried. "You started this. Now come on, Dad, cough it up."

He reached into his suit-jacket pocket and dropped a set of keys into her hand. "Okay. There you go. Happy birthday!"

Melissa stared down at the keys, confused. "What's this?"

"Look." He pulled open the front door. Sitting in the drive was a shiny blue Pontiac Firebird.

"Are you kidding?" Melissa cried, finally catching on. "That's for *me?*"

He just grinned and nodded his head.

"I don't believe it!" Melissa jumped up and hugged him, nearly knocking him over backward. Then she pushed open the screen door and ran out to examine her new car.

"Well, go ahead. Sit in it," Mr. Dryden said after they had walked around it at least a dozen times.

"I can't believe this is mine," Melissa said, sliding behind the wheel. She sniffed, smiling as she breathed in that wonderful new car smell. She ran her hand over the leather seat and then tried the steering wheel.

"I may want to borrow it from time to time," her father said, lowering his bulky frame into the passenger seat.

"Listen, Dad, this is too much."

"What do you mean?"

"You know what I mean. This is too extravagant."

He laughed. "Yeah. You're a spoiled brat. You're spoiled rotten. Maybe I'll keep the car after all."

He grabbed the keys from her hand, but she grabbed them back. "On second thought, what's so terrible about being spoiled rotten?" she said.

He sighed. His smile faded. "When I was your age, I was lucky to get a toy car. Birthdays were pretty grim around my house."

"I know, I know. Your mother couldn't afford a

birthday cake. So she used to buy stale birthday cakes that other people forgot to pick up. On your third birthday you told everyone your name was Seymour because that's what it said on your cake."

He shook his head. "You know all my old jokes. Listen, it just makes me feel good to be able to give you nice gifts. It makes me realize how far I've come from those days."

She kissed him on the cheek. "I've got to show this to Della. Can I drive it?"

He shrugged and started to lift himself out of the car. "It's yours. Go ahead. But don't stay too long. Your mother will be disappointed if she doesn't get to see it."

"Great! Della won't believe this!" She ran into the house, got her purse with her driver's license in it, and ran back to the car. Mr. Dryden was still in the drive, polishing a spot on the hood with his jacket sleeve.

She climbed behind the wheel and carefully closed the door. "You look great in it," her father said. "Your hair looks like it's already blowing in the wind even though you're not moving yet!"

"Very funny, Dad. Remind me to laugh when I get home." Why was everybody always putting her hair down? She turned the key in the ignition. The car began to purr. She turned to the rear window and started to back down the drive, slowly, carefully.

He's standing there watching me. I know I'm going to back right into the hedges, she told herself, realiz-

14

ing she was really nervous driving a beautiful new car.

But she made it past the hedges and onto Fear Street. A few minutes later she turned up The Mill Road and headed toward the North Hills section of town where Della lived.

The car handled beautifully. It was so easy to drive. The Mill Road was pretty crowded, with people going home from work, but most of the traffic was heading the other way. The sun was low behind the trees, but the air was still warm and humid.

She turned onto Canyon Drive to get away from the traffic and pressed down hard on the accelerator. The car responded immediately with a roar and a burst of speed.

Wait till Buddy gets a load of this, she thought, passing a slow-moving vegetable truck, then swerving back into the right lane. Wait till *everyone* gets a load of this!

She glanced at the speedometer—she was doing seventy-five—so she lightened up on the gas pedal. She was driving right into the sun now. Lowering the visor helped a little but didn't cut all of the glare.

"Oh!"

She cried out as the car suddenly veered to the right.

Melissa grabbed the wheel tighter, her heart pounding.

What had happened? Was the car pulling to the right? No. It happened so suddenly, with such force that it felt as if someone had grabbed the wheel.

15

She felt a sudden chill. She put her hand over the air vent to see if the air conditioner was blowing. It wasn't. Bright sunlight blanketed the windshield, and yet the air in the car was extremely cold.

Melissa slowed down, keeping a tight grip on the wheel. She had just started to relax a little when the car jerked again, swerving wildly to the right. The tires spun onto the soft shoulder. Melissa struggled to regain control.

What was going on?

Again it felt as if someone had jerked the steering wheel.

She tightened her grip on the wheel and leaned forward. She slowed down to twenty-five. There's something wrong with the car, she told herself.

What was that?

It sounded like whispering. A voice. Nearby. No. It couldn't be. It was the wind.

Again she heard it. She shivered from the cold, from surprise, from sudden fear. She gripped the wheel tighter still and stared straight ahead.

What was it saying? She could hear it so clearly. A whisper right in her ear. Did it say her name?

Yes. That's what it sounded like.

Melissssssssssa. Just wind. Cold wind in her ear. Cold wind whispering so softly in her ear.

Melissssssssssa . . .

Della's house was just a few blocks away.

I can make it, she thought, staring straight ahead,

16

ignoring the whispering wind that repeated her name so insistently, so menacingly.

I can make it. If I can just keep control of the car . . .

"No!" she cried as the car swerved hard, this time to the left, crossing the center lane into the path of an onrushing oil truck.

chapter

3

"*H*appy birthday, Lissa."

"Hi, Della. You're late. Everyone's here already."

It was Friday evening. Melissa's house was filled with kids. Della stepped into the front hallway. There was a loud crash from the den, followed by laughter. "Sounds like I'm just in time," Della said, handing Melissa a present: a flat, rectangular box wrapped in red and blue tissue paper. "It's a car," she said. "I thought you could use two."

"Don't mention my new car," Melissa said, rolling her eyes. "Only two days old and in the garage already."

"Did they find out what's wrong with the steering?"

"No. They can't find anything wrong. Daddy told them to keep looking till they find it. He's more upset than I am. And I'm the one who was almost killed by that oil truck. Hey—where's Pete?"

"Here I am." Pete Goodwin popped up behind Della, a broad smile on his handsome face. "Happy birthday." He handed Melissa a small, flat package, obviously a CD. "Hope you like Weird Al."

"Oh, get real, Pete," Della said, poking him hard in the ribs with her elbow. "It isn't Weird Al," she told Melissa.

Pete shrugged. "Della told me you were into Weird Al."

"I'll put it in the other room with the other stuff," Melissa said.

Pete's okay, she thought. For a long time she had wondered why Della liked him so much. Sure, he was nice looking. But he was so straight and preppie, and he always seemed sort of snobby and stiff.

Here he was in his standard outfit—tan chinos and a white pullover shirt with the little black Polo pony on the breast. His wavy brown hair was short and perfectly parted. He looked like such a preppie.

But after spending a lot of time with Pete and Della, Melissa had decided her first impressions of Pete were wrong. He was really nice and very smart, and he loosened up a lot after he got to know you.

Della, of course, looked as beautiful as ever. Her straight black hair, tied loosely by a plain white ribbon, fell softly down her back. Her silky green blouse matched her eyes. Her black, straight-legged jeans showed off her perfect model's figure.

Melissa tugged at both sides of her frizzy blond hair, which she had actually tried to brush before the party. I'm not going to be jealous of Della, she thought, staring at Della's hair as she followed them into the large and noisy den. I'm not going to be jealous—not on my birthday.

"Hey, Lissa—good party!" Marnie Foster called. The stereo was cranked up really loud, and she was dancing in the middle of the crowded room with Billy Clawson.

Billy was such a bad dancer. He looked like a penguin bobbing from side to side. Melissa had dated Billy for a while in her freshman year. Watching him flop around to the music with Marnie, she couldn't imagine why!

"You got any more chips?" David Metcalfe called. He was sitting in an armchair in the corner, holding the potato-chip bowl in his lap, stuffing his face.

Krissie Munroe reached out from behind the armchair, grabbed the potato-chip bowl, and dumped it over David's head. He protested loudly and blindly reached for Krissie. But she was already halfway across the room.

"Hey—where's Buddy?" Della asked, leaning close to Melissa and shouting to be heard over the music.

Good question, Melissa thought.

"He's late," she shouted. "So what else is new?" Buddy wasn't the most punctual person in the universe. But Melissa was disappointed that he hadn't tried to be on time for her birthday party. She looked around the room and realized Buddy would be the last to arrive.

Can he still be mad at me about the other night? she

wondered, glancing up at the clock over the mantel-piece.

No, he had been very apologetic. And he had called her the next day, and they'd had a nice long talk.

Stop being so nervous, she scolded herself. It isn't even that late.

She thought she heard the doorbell. It was impossible to hear anything over the loud music and the even louder voices. She started out of the den, and there was Buddy, grinning at her from the doorway.

He was wearing a sleeveless blue T-shirt and white tennis shorts, obviously showing off his tan. He looks great, Melissa thought, rushing up to greet him. "Hi." He kissed her quickly and shoved a small box, wrapped in silver, into her hand. "Go ahead. Open it."

"No." She squeezed his hand. "I'll open it later."

"With all the others?" He gave her his hurt look.

She leaned against him and whispered in his ear. "Stay after everyone's left. I'll open it then."

"Hey, Buddy—" David Metcalfe yelled from the chair. "Bet I know what *you're* giving Melissa for her birthday!" He said it real suggestively, with a dirty leer on his face, and everyone laughed.

"Shut up, Metcalfe!" Buddy shouted. But he was laughing too. Melissa punched him playfully on the chest, and he staggered backward.

"Any more chips?" Metcalfe called, holding up the empty bowl.

"Turn the music up!" someone yelled. "I can still hear Metcalfe!"

21

Marnie Foster had gone over by the window to talk to friends, but Billy Clawson was still dancing—all by himself. He pulled Krissie Munroe into the center of the room, but she stood and stared at him, refusing to dance. It didn't seem to bother Billy, who didn't slow down, holding on to both of Krissie's hands as he bobbed about. Finally Krissie's boyfriend, Ira Hewlitt, came over to rescue her.

A slow number came on, and a few more couples started dancing. Melissa had to laugh. Pete was standing straight as a broomstick as he danced with Della. She had her eyes closed and didn't seem to mind.

Melissa looked for Buddy, thinking he might want to dance. But he was in a corner talking heatedly to Normie Shrader. They were both demonstrating forehand swings, so Melissa figured they were talking tennis, which both of them were fanatics about.

The party was going really well. Everyone seemed to be having a great time. Melissa relaxed and enjoyed it too. The next time she looked at the clock it was past eleven-thirty.

Uh-oh, she thought. She had promised she'd try to have everyone out of the house by midnight. "Cake time!" she cried, and turned off the stereo. "Cake time! Come on. Everybody into the dining room."

"You sure know how to spoil a party!" David Metcalfe yelled.

Everyone hissed him down.

"Just for that, I'm not going to sing," David grumbled.

Having them all sing "Happy Birthday" to her was just as embarrassing on her seventeenth birthday as it had been on all the others. But the huge chocolate cake was moist and delicious, and Billy Clawson was the only one to spill his soda all over the tablecloth, so Melissa considered this part of the party a success.

"Aren't we going to play pin the tail on the donkey?" Krissie asked as they finished their cake.

"Aren't we going to play spin the bottle?" David Metcalfe asked with a dirty laugh.

"Hey—remember post office? Did you ever play that when you were a kid?" Pete asked.

"I played it last week," Billy said, and everyone laughed.

"How about dirty doctor?" Melissa asked.

"Great game! Great game!" everyone agreed.

"My dad's a doctor," Normie said, "so I used to play it with a real stethoscope!"

"Whoooo!" "Wow!" Everyone seemed really impressed.

"How do you play?" Marnie asked innocently.

That got the biggest laugh of the night.

Billy jumped up and started to pull her away from the table. "Come in the other room. I'll show you. I'll even let *you* be the patient!"

This got an even bigger laugh.

"No time!" Melissa cried, swallowing her last mouthful of cake and jumping to her feet. "You've all got to be out of here ten minutes ago!"

23

"Party pooper!" someone yelled.

"Open the presents!" David shouted.

"Open the presents! Open the presents!" a few of her friends took up the chant.

"Okay. Sorry. I almost forgot."

"Sure. You already got a car. Why should you care about *our* presents?" Buddy said.

Nice, Buddy. Melissa knew he was only joking, but for some reason, the joke annoyed her. Her friends often gave her a hard time because her family was wealthy. They were always making cracks. She didn't expect to hear them from Buddy too.

"Come on. I put them all in the downstairs guest bedroom," Melissa said. "We'll have to hurry. My parents will be home soon, and I promised you'd be out of here when they got back."

"We can take a hint," David said.

Buddy put his arm around her shoulders as she led them to the guest bedroom. She immediately forgave him for his stupid remark.

"I stacked all the presents on the bed," Melissa said to no one in particular, "and I think we can—"

She clicked on the light, looked at the bed, and gasped.

"Oh, no!"

Everyone pushed into the room. "What's going on?"

"What happened?"

"Who did that?"

The room grew silent as everyone stared at the bed.

24

The presents were scattered over the bed and floor. They had all been ripped open.

Melissa was kissing Buddy good night in the den when her parents walked in.

"The party's still going on?" Mrs. Dryden asked.

Buddy, embarrassed, pulled away from Melissa and jumped up from the couch. "I was just . . . uh . . . going."

"How was the party?" Mr. Dryden asked, walking over to the potato-chip bowl, visibly disappointed to find it empty.

"Great!" Melissa said quickly. She had decided not to tell her parents about the presents being ripped open. Why bother them with something so silly. "I think everyone had a good time."

"Yeah, it was great," Buddy repeated, inching toward the front hall. "Too bad about your rug. And the wallpaper. And those dishes."

"What?" Melissa's mother looked as if she were about to have a heart attack.

"Buddy's kidding, Mom," Melissa said, walking over and giving Buddy a hard shove. "Aren't you used to his bizarre sense of humor yet?"

"I don't think I'll ever get used to it," Mrs. Dryden said, slumping into a chair.

"Did they eat *all* the potato chips?" Mr. Dryden asked, turning another large plastic bowl upside down.

"When the potato chips ran out, they ate the bowls," Buddy said.

"Buddy—go home," Melissa groaned.

"Where'd you get that beautiful silver pendant?" Mrs. Dryden asked, walking over and lifting it off Melissa's neck to examine it more closely.

"Buddy gave it to me."

"Very nice." Mrs. Dryden looked at Buddy as if seeing him for the first time. "What good taste. Did someone help you pick it out, Buddy?"

"Good night, everyone," Buddy said and made a hasty exit.

"Strange kid," Mrs. Dryden muttered.

"What?" Melissa asked.

"Beautiful pendant," her mother said, lifting it up and turning it over to read the back.

"Mom—please! You're choking me!"

After telling them a few more details about the party and thanking them for letting her take over the house, Melissa went upstairs to bed. She got undressed, pulled on her father's old pajama shirt that she had failed to return, clicked off the lamp, and slid under the covers, feeling tired but not sleepy.

The window was open. It was a cool night, the first hint that autumn was on its way. A gentle breeze blew the curtains out, then they fell back. The air smelled sweet and fresh.

The streetlight at the end of the yard cast a yellow light in the room. Melissa stared at the moving shadows on the wall. Who could have done it? she wondered. Who could have ripped apart her presents and left them strewn all over the room?

Her friends all seemed terribly shocked by the sight

in the guest bedroom. She hadn't seen any of them leave the den or living room. Besides, they were her friends, all people who liked her. No one there would do anything that mean to her. The only other person in the house was Marta, the housekeeper. But she was busy in the kitchen, working to keep the food for the party coming, and washing the plates and glasses. It couldn't have been Marta.

Then who?

And more importantly, why? Why would someone sneak into the bedroom and tear open every package? To ruin the party? Just to make Melissa feel bad?

It made no sense, no sense at all.

Melissa ran her hand over the silver pendant Buddy had given her. It felt cool and smooth in her hand. I'm going to wear it all the time, she thought. I'm never going to take it off.

Even her mother had been impressed by it.

Suddenly the room felt cold again. I guess I'd better close the window, Melissa thought. She sat up and started to climb out of bed. Such a chilling cold to come on so suddenly.

She lowered her bare feet to the carpet and looked up.

A young man stepped out of the shadows at the foot of her bed. She couldn't see his face. The light from the window formed an outline around his dark form. She could see that he had long, dark hair, narrow shoulders.

He had no face. Only the blackness of night where his face should have been.

27

"Who are you? What are you doing here?" she cried.

He didn't reply. He moved around the bed, walking slowly toward her.

The Fear Street Prowler, she thought.

She drew in her breath and screamed at the top of her lungs.

chapter
4

As the dark figure moved closer, his features remained hidden in shadow. It looked to Melissa, grasping the bed sheet with both hands, choked with fear, as if he had no features at all. No features, no face.

His head, his arms, his whole body came out of the shadows and now were part of the shadow. And that shadow was moving forward, arms raised, to engulf her.

"Melissa—what on earth!"

Her father burst into the room, stumbling over her sneakers, which she had tossed by the door. He caught his balance and fumbled for the lamp switch.

"He's in here, Daddy! He's in here!" Melissa managed to cry out in a tight voice she didn't recognize.

Finally the light came on. Her father stood against

the wall, his face filled with confusion, frantically looking around the room.

"Where, Lissa?"

"He's here! He's—"

"Who?" Seeing no one, her father started to breathe normally. He walked over to her bed and slumped down on the edge.

"Daddy, he—"

"I don't see anyone."

"What happened? Why did she scream again?" Mrs. Dryden came into the room. She was still dressed, hadn't even taken off her shoes.

Melissa climbed out of bed. "I'm not crazy! Someone was in this room."

Mr. Dryden stood up and walked quickly to the window. "Did he jump out the window?" He looked out, leaning far over the window ledge.

"Wes, don't lean out like that!" Mrs. Dryden called, clutching at her throat, frightened.

He pulled his head back in and turned to Melissa, who was standing right beside him. He shook his head. "I don't see anyone."

"Who was in here? A man? What did he look like? Call the police, Wes." Mrs. Dryden walked over to the window to pull her husband to the phone.

"How can I call the police? There's no one here." He looked skeptically at Melissa.

"He . . . he disappeared," Melissa said uncertainly. "I saw him. He was as close to me as you are. I saw him clearly. I didn't make it up. I wasn't dreaming."

"And then he disappeared into thin air?" Her father pushed his glasses up on his nose.

"I—I don't know."

"Well, what did he look like? Can you describe him?" her mother demanded.

"Well . . . he . . ." Melissa's mouth dropped open. She pulled absent-mindedly at a curly strand of hair as she thought. "It was too dark," she said finally. "I couldn't see his face. I could just see—"

"What? What could you see?" her mother asked.

"I could see that he had long hair."

"And?"

"That's all," Melissa said quietly. She knew it sounded stupid. But it was the truth. Why were they doubting her? Why wouldn't they believe what she was telling them? Couldn't they see how frightened she was?

Her father walked over to comfort her, as if reading her mind. He hugged her. "You've got to control your imagination," he said softly, smoothing her hair with one hand. "Last time—"

"Last time was a tree branch," Melissa said, becoming impatient with them and letting it show in her voice. "Tonight was real." She pulled away from her father and walked to the window and sat down on the windowsill. The night air felt cool against her back.

"If he was real, where is he?" Her mother just wouldn't let up. "Why can't you describe him?"

"I *told* you, Mother," she said angrily. "It was too dark. I could only see his outline. He raised his arms. He moved toward me. And then Daddy came in."

31

"And he vanished into thin air." Mrs. Dryden shook her head. "It's just the excitement over your birthday, the new car. It all caught up with you, that's all. It's perfectly understandable."

"Please, Mother. Don't talk to me like I'm a baby."

"Come on, Lissa." Mr. Dryden held out his arms. "There's no need to be angry at us."

"You don't believe me, do you?" Melissa snapped.

"Well, no," her father said, glancing at her mother. "I think this is all power of suggestion."

"What?"

"I think the stories about the Fear Street Prowler have upset you, upset you enough to think that you're seeing him in your room. I believe that you really saw what you said you saw. But I think your mind was playing tricks on you. I think—"

"That I'm crazy?"

"No. Of course not," her mother broke in. "Let me make you some warm milk. It will make you feel sleepy."

Melissa sighed. There was no way she was going to convince her parents that she wasn't imagining the shadowy intruder. "Good night, you two," she said wearily. She gave them a tired wave and climbed back into bed. "I'm feeling calm now. I'm sorry I disturbed you."

Her mother started out the door, looking very troubled. Her father followed, but stopped at the doorway and turned back. "Shall I close the window? Will that make you feel better?"

Melissa shook her head. "The breeze feels nice. It's the first cool night we've had."

"Shall I turn off the lamp?"

"Yeah. Thanks. 'Night, Daddy. 'Night, Mom."

They muttered good night and walked out into the hall. A few seconds later Melissa could hear her parents talking about her in their room across the hall.

She stared up at the ceiling. It seemed to be glowing, pale yellow from the light coming in through the window.

I'm wide-awake now, she thought. Wide-awake. I'll never get to sleep tonight.

She sat up, then climbed out of bed. It was so bright in her room. She didn't remember the streetlight being that bright before. The breeze blew the curtains into the room, allowing even more light in.

Impulsively, she walked to the window and pulled the curtains to the side. The air felt so refreshing, so soft and cool.

Resting her hands lightly on the window ledge, she leaned out. It was such a clear night, she could see all the way down Fear Street. Through the trees that lined both sides of the narrow street, she could almost make out the jagged outlines of Simon Fear's burned-out old mansion at the far end of the street.

Melissa's friends were always telling her terrible stories about Fear Street. But she loved the neighborhood. Her parents loved antiques and rambling Victorian houses and anything old and interesting, and they had passed their enthusiasm on to Melissa. Fear

Street is by far the most interesting street in Shadyside, she thought.

Looking up, she saw the full moon. It seemed just a few yards above her head. Its pale light reflected off the silver pendant around her neck. She lifted the pendant and stared at the shimmering moonlight in it. How beautiful, she thought.

She dropped the pendant and stretched farther out the window, leaning on both hands. What was that scampering across the grass in the yard across the street? Was it a rabbit?

I'd better get back to bed, she thought. I'll be totally wrecked tomorrow.

But as she started to straighten up, she felt two powerful hands on her back. Before she could resist or cry out, the two hands shoved her, shoved her hard from behind, shoved her with startling, almost inhuman power.

chapter
5

*T*he hands pushed hard against her back. She would have sailed out the window if she hadn't made a desperate grab for the sides of the window frame.

Gripping the frame tightly, she regained her balance and pushed back, resisting the steady force on her back.

Her attacker shoved even harder.

The hands felt so cold on her back. The air felt so cold.

She sucked in her breath and pushed back with all her might against the wooden window frame, resisting the attack, refusing to fall.

Gathering all her strength, she whirled around and turned to face him.

There was no one there.

She stared into the darkness of her room, panting loudly, each breath a cry of pain, of terror, of relief.

Where are you? she thought. Where did you go? How did you disappear so quickly?

He must still be in the room. But where?

He had no time to hide, to duck out of sight.

Instead of feeling calmer, she felt the fear begin to grow. Her legs trembled. She felt sick to her stomach. She was covered in a cold sweat.

"Hey—I know you're here!" she called, her voice a choked whisper.

Somehow she made it to the bed and turned on the lamp. Her eyes darted quickly around the room. No one was there.

"I know you're here."

On trembling legs she walked to the closet and slid open both doors. No one.

She could still feel the cold on her back. She could still feel the hands pushing her with such force, with such evil determination.

"I know you're here."

She dropped to the floor and looked under the bed. No one.

Should she call for her dad? No. He would only come running in to find the room empty once again. She'd get those looks again, those looks from both her parents that said they were starting to think there was something seriously wrong with her.

Well, was there?

Was she cracking up?

36

She sat on the carpet and leaned back against the bed. She stared up through the open window at the yellow full moon.

I almost went flying out that window, she thought. Someone tried to push me out that window. I didn't imagine it. I didn't dream it.

I'm not cracking up.

Still feeling trembly, she pulled herself back into bed. She drew the covers up to her chin and waited for the shaking to stop. There's no one here, she thought. I'm safe now. Perfectly safe.

A few minutes later she fell asleep with the light on.

When a cold shadow drifted up to her bed and hovered over her, she didn't awaken, didn't see it.

Buddy tossed a rake onto his driveway, then a long-handled broom, and a shovel. "Look out," he warned Melissa. He heaved an unopened bag of potting soil out next.

"Why are you throwing that stuff around?" Melissa asked, making her way across the drive and into the garage.

"I'm not throwing it around. I'm throwing it out of the garage."

"Why?"

"So I can carry it all back in. That's called Cleaning the Garage."

"Didn't you just clean the garage a few weeks ago?" She moved aside as he tossed a wooden basket containing garden trowels and pruning shears onto the drive.

"Yeah. But my dad said I didn't do a good enough job. I wasn't thorough enough. So today I'm being thorough."

"You're tossing everything out, then bringing everything back in?"

"Yeah. But neatly. Look out." He tried to heave a rolled-up garden hose, but it unraveled, and he had to drag it out. He dropped it into the wheelbarrow and returned for more stuff.

He was wearing a stained, plain white T-shirt and faded jean cutoffs, white tennis sneakers with no socks. He looks great, Melissa thought. "You should keep that tan all-year-round," she said.

He laughed. "Yeah. Maybe I'll go to one of those tanning places every week and barbecue myself." He picked up a large bag of fertilizer and carried it out to the driveway.

"You didn't notice that I'm wearing your pendant," she said, running her hand over it.

"Sure, I noticed." He wiped the sweat off his forehead with his arm. "Go on with what you were telling me on the phone earlier."

She grabbed the handlebars of his bike and leaned against them. "Nothing more to tell. There was someone in my room. And my parents both think I'm crazy."

She waited for him to say something, but he only picked up an aluminum ladder and started to carry it past her.

"You think I'm crazy too?"

He didn't answer until he had carried the ladder

out, set it down on the grass, and walked back in. "Maybe it was the wind. Or shadows or something."

"Shadows don't push you out windows," she snapped angrily. She shoved the bike against the wall, turned, and crossed her arms over her chest. "I'm not crazy, Buddy."

He put down the crate he was carrying and went over to her. He put a dirty hand on her shoulder. "I'm just trying to figure out what it could be."

"Me too," she said, moving out from under his hand. "And what about the birthday presents? I just keep seeing them, all ripped up like that. Who could've done such a stupid, horrible thing?"

He shrugged. "I don't know."

"I'm kind of frightened," she admitted. "It's all too weird."

"You have to chill out."

"What's that mean?" she snapped. Then she realized she had no reason to be angry at Buddy. He was trying so hard to be sympathetic and understanding. "Sorry," she said, nuzzling her face against his sweaty T-shirt. "I—I just wish they'd catch that Fear Street Prowler. I keep thinking he's going to come climbing in my window and—"

"What makes you think he'll come to your house?"

"I don't know. I have such weird thoughts sometimes. I mean, I think maybe he's already been in my house."

Buddy shook his head. "Oh, right. For sure. He climbed in the window, opened all your birthday presents, and left. That makes a lot of sense."

She playfully pushed him away with both hands. "Thanks for all the support. I've got to run."

"Where to?"

"I promised Della I'd meet her at the mall. I have a little money. I thought maybe I'd buy some clothes for school."

"School? Don't remind me. Only a few more days of freedom."

"I'm kind of looking forward to it," Melissa said, stepping carefully over all of the stuff strewn in the drive. "Aren't you?"

"Huh? And give up all the excitement of cleaning out the garage? Get real!"

"See you later. What time are you picking me up?"

He scratched his forehead, leaving black streaks across it. "Hey, why don't you pick *me* up? You're the one with the awesome car."

She laughed. "I knew you were going to say that. Okay. Pick you up at eight—if my car is fixed and out of the garage." She climbed into her mother's Volvo station wagon and, feeling a little cheered up, gave Buddy a farewell wave. But he had already disappeared back into the garage.

"That looks great on you," Della said. She reached over and squeezed the material of the wine-colored sweater. "It sort of fills you out."

"What's that supposed to mean?" Melissa asked, frowning at herself in the full-length mirror.

"Stop being so sensitive," Della said, picking up the same sweater in light brown.

"I'm a very sensitive person," Melissa said in a highfalutin, pretentious voice.

"You're also skinny as a rail," Della said.

Melissa shot her a dirty look.

"What do you think of these?" Krissie asked, stepping out of the dressing booth in a pair of straight-legged black corduroy jeans. Krissie had bumped into Melissa and Della just outside the Clothes Closet and invited herself to tag along with them. She tossed back her wavy, black hair and made her way to the mirror to examine herself.

"They're tight enough," Della said, rolling her eyes for Melissa's benefit.

"They look great," Melissa told Krissie.

"Maybe a size smaller," Krissie said, studying herself from every angle.

"You'd be arrested," Melissa said. All three of them laughed. A serious-looking salesgirl across the store looked up to see what was so funny.

Krissie admired herself a while longer. "You think these are *too* sexy?"

"You're just fishing for a compliment," Melissa said, laughing. "No. They're not sexy at all."

"You're lying. I think I'll buy two pairs. Oh, wow," she said suddenly, pointing to a girl who had just entered the store. "Do you believe what that girl is wearing? Are those plastic pedal pushers?"

"I think they're fake leather or something," Della said. She disappeared into the dressing booth with an armload of clothes.

Krissie couldn't get over the girl across the store.

"And look at that tacky top with the fringe. Oh, no. I don't *believe* the white plastic boots!"

"Hey, I know her," Melissa said, watching the girl go through a stack of faded jeans on a table. "Her name's Marylou. I forget her last name. She was at my day camp when I was little."

"Someone should *send* her to camp in that tacky outfit!" Krissie said.

Melissa didn't laugh. "She's just poor, that's all."

"Huh? What do you mean?"

"Don't you know what *poor* means, Krissie? It means she doesn't have much money. Her family lives over in the Old Village. She has a whole bunch of brothers and sisters. She probably can't afford nice clothes."

"Being poor is in bad taste," Krissie said and then laughed at her own joke.

"Not funny," Melissa said disgustedly. "I don't ever want to be a rich snob who turns up her nose at people."

"Save the lecture," Krissie muttered, heading back to the dressing booths. "I'm sorry, okay?"

Melissa followed her. "We're so lucky that our parents are well-off," she said. "But it's just luck. You and I didn't do anything. We didn't earn it."

"Really, Melissa. If you want to give a sermon, why don't you go to church?" Krissie jerked the dressing-booth curtain shut.

Melissa realized she might have gone too far. But she meant what she had said. Sometimes she felt really uncomfortable having so much more than other kids. She wondered what those other kids must think of her, how much they resented her for being so lucky.

A few hours later she was thinking about all this as she drove home. After dropping Della off in North Hills, she headed the Volvo wagon down Park Drive toward Fear Street. I'll have to apologize to Krissie, she decided. I had no business lecturing her like that. I'm just so edgy these days.

"You're overtired." That's what her mother would say.

Melissa laughed to herself. But her laugh was cut short by the whispering sound. Again. The sound of air, whispering her name.

"Melisssssssssa."

"Oh!" she cried out.

"Melisssssssssssa."

No. Not again. What on earth could be making that sound?

The station wagon suddenly felt cold, the same chilling, damp cold she had felt in her new car.

"Melissssssssssssa."

And suddenly there he was, in the passenger seat beside her.

A young man, probably about her age. Tough looking. With black, greasy hair down to his collar. And dark, dangerous eyes. Dressed all in blue denim.

Melissa cried out, and crashed into the car ahead of her.

chapter
_____
6

The driver of the car Melissa hit—a
large, middle-aged man in a gray business suit—came
storming out of his car, red-faced and angry. Melissa,
somewhat stunned, didn't move until he tapped on
her window, three hard taps with the back of his hand.

She rolled down the window, but didn't get out.
"Weren't you watching?" the man asked, his face
growing even redder. "I was stopped for the light."

"Sorry," Melissa said, starting to feel a little more
normal. "Are you okay?"

"Why didn't you stop?" the man demanded angrily,
ignoring her question. "Are you stoned or something?" He stared at her, examining her eyes.

"No. I just didn't see—I mean, this boy popped up
beside me and I was so surprised—"

"Boy?" The man leaned down to the window and

peered past Melissa to the passenger side. She could smell his aftershave, which was sharp and sweet. "What boy?"

Melissa turned to the passenger seat, then raised herself up so she could see the backseat. There was no one there.

"Hey—where are you?" she cried aloud. "Where'd you go?" She turned back to the man. "I'm sorry. He was here. Really. And—"

He threw up his hands impatiently. "I can't listen to this nonsense. I'm late for a meeting." He left her window to go examine his rear bumper. Melissa reluctantly pushed open the car door and stepped outside. She felt a little shaky from the jolt of hitting the other car. She took a few steps and began to feel better.

"*Your* car isn't even dented," the man said, rubbing his chin, his face still nearly tomato red.

"And what about your car?" Melissa asked, thinking about the boy with the long hair. The boy looked so tough, so angry. She could see that even in the brief glimpse she got of him. Have I seen him some place before? she wondered.

"Just a scratch," the man said, getting down on his knees to look under the rear of the car. "I guess we're both okay."

"My parents have insurance."

He climbed to his feet and dusted off the knees of his trousers even though they were clean. "No need. Let's just forget about this, okay?" He smiled for the first time. His face started to return to a normal color. He stretched and rolled his head around. "Neck seems to be okay. Guess we were lucky."

"I guess," Melissa said doubtfully. "I'm really sorry. You're being so nice about this."

"I'm a nice guy," he said flatly, getting back into his car. "Do me a favor, though, okay? Drive behind someone else from now on."

"Oh. Sure." Melissa wasn't certain if he was joking or not. She watched him pull away, thinking about the long-haired boy. She could see him so clearly, his dark eyes, his nervous frown. She *couldn't* have imagined him.

"Hey—move it!"

Melissa looked up to see two cars behind her, the drivers poking their heads out of their windows.

"Hey, miss, are you okay? Didn't you hear us honking?"

Startled, she jumped into the station wagon, pulled the door closed, and drove away. She hadn't heard the horns at all. She hadn't heard anything. I was in my own world, she thought. My own dreamworld where boys appear and disappear, and the wind whispers my name. . . .

"I'm really worried about you, Lissa. You're obviously extremely—"

"No, I'm not overtired, Mother." Melissa tore a piece off her roll but didn't eat it. She hadn't intended to tell her parents about the car accident at dinner, but during a long silence, she had just blurted it out. Now she was really sorry she had told them.

"This young man you say you saw," her father asked thoughtfully, wiping sauce off his chin with his dinner napkin, "did he look like the young man you claimed you saw in your room last night?"

"Don't say *claimed*. Why'd you have to say *claimed?*" Melissa shrieked, sounding more angry than she intended. "You really think I'm crazy, don't you? You think I'm some kind of nut case! Claimed! Claimed! That's the kind of thing you say to someone in one of your court cases, Daddy. I'm not your client. I'm your daughter!"

She knew she had gone too far. She couldn't help it. It was so infuriating that they both refused to believe her.

"Calm down, dear. Try to eat." Mrs. Dryden hated scenes of any kind, especially at the dinner table.

"I'm sorry. I didn't mean . . ." Her father pulled off his glasses and rubbed the bridge of his nose. His eyes looked so much smaller with his glasses off. He suddenly looked very tired.

"Your dad had a really good idea this afternoon," Mrs. Dryden said to Melissa, finishing the last piece of salmon on her plate.

Here she goes, changing the subject again, Melissa thought. For once, however, Melissa was relieved.

"Why don't you tell her?" Mrs. Dryden urged her husband.

Mr. Dryden swallowed a mouthful of scalloped

potatoes. "Excellent dinner tonight. Remind me to compliment Marta."

"I hear you. Thanks for the compliment!" Marta called through the closed kitchen door.

Mr. and Mrs. Dryden laughed.

Marta probably thinks I'm crazy too, Melissa thought gloomily.

"Go ahead. Tell Melissa your idea," her mother urged.

"Well, your mom and I have to go to this lawyers' convention," Mr. Dryden started. "It's next weekend in Las Vegas. We're leaving Thursday night to make it a long weekend. And I thought maybe you'd like to come too."

"It'll be really good for you," her mother said quickly, before Melissa had a chance to react. "You need a change of scenery. School doesn't start until the following week, so it's the perfect time to go, and—"

"I really don't want to," Melissa interrupted.

"Well, we really think—" her mother started.

"Why not, Lissa?" Mr. Dryden asked, very disappointed.

"I just don't want to go all the way to Las Vegas with a bunch of lawyers. It wouldn't be any fun for me. What would I do while you and Mom are in your meetings and going to parties? I'm not old enough to go to the casinos. I'd have to hang around the hotel waiting for you."

"But, Melissa," Mrs. Dryden argued, "there's tennis, and swimming, and all the shows. I really think you'd have a great time. You need to get out of this house."

"Sorry," Melissa said, tossing down her napkin and getting up from the table. "No way. No thanks."

"Where are you going?" Mrs. Dryden asked, not bothering to hide her anger at Melissa's refusal to accompany them.

"I have a date with Buddy. I'm picking him up. He'll be so surprised to see my new car is back." Impulsively, she leaned over and gave her father a quick kiss on the forehead. "Thanks for picking it up for me, Daddy." He smiled up at her, a forgiving smile.

"I really think you should reconsider," Mrs. Dryden called. Melissa didn't reply, but hurried up to her room to get changed.

She showered quickly, then put on a red, ribbed sweater with fringe along the hem and a new pair of jeans. She was putting Buddy's silver pendant around her neck, struggling with the clasp, when the boy appeared beside her.

He seemed to be off-balance at first, but he quickly got his bearings, and his dark eyes stared into hers. She could see him clearly now. He had dark brown hair that looked as if it hadn't been washed in weeks. It was parted haphazardly in the middle and hung down past his collar. He had thick, dark eyebrows, high cheekbones, and a mouth that seemed to fall naturally into an unpleasant sneer. He was wearing a faded blue denim jacket and blue denim jeans.

49

To Melissa's surprise, she wasn't frightened this time. This time she felt only anger.

"Who are you?" she demanded, taking a step toward him.

He seemed surprised by her boldness, but didn't reply. He looked her up and down, being very obvious about it.

"You made me dent my mom's car," she said.

He shrugged his narrow shoulders as if to say who cares. "So? You can just buy another one—right?" he said bitterly.

His voice was higher, softer than she'd imagined.

"Who are you?" she repeated, staring back at him, refusing to blink, to back down. "How did you get in my room? In my car?"

Her anger seemed to amuse him. He looked past her to the window. Then he walked over to her dressing table and stared down at her makeup and the other items.

"You don't remember me?"

He stepped toward her again.

"No. Why should I remember you?" she asked, feeling the fear return.

"You should remember me," he said, rushing forward and pushing his face up close to hers. "You should remember me—you killed me!"

chapter
7

She backed away from him, and tripped on her sneakers and fell over backward.

He put his hands on his hips and smiled down at her, obviously enjoying seeing her helpless on the floor like that. She saw that he had tattoos on the back of his right hand, but she couldn't make out what they were.

"Let me up."

He sneered again. "Get up. I'm not stopping you."

Melissa rolled to the right and jumped to her feet. They stared at each other across her bed. "I've never seen you before," she said.

He tossed his head, then smoothed back his greasy hair. "Convenient memory," he muttered bitterly.

"I don't know what you're talking about. Stop being so mysterious."

He seemed to find that very funny. "I'm not being mysterious. I told you flat out—you killed me. Take a good look. Remember me now?"

"You're crazy. If you're dead, how can you be standing here now? What are you—a ghost?"

What should she do? Run from the room? Call for her father? No. She wanted some answers from this strange intruder. She wanted to find out what was going on once and for all.

"Don't play innocent." He turned his back on her. "You mean to say that you killed me and didn't even notice? You mean you're so rich that—"

"I didn't kill you!" Melissa screamed. "If I killed you, how did I do it?"

His hands coiled into fists. He remained with his back to her. "I don't remember," he said in a flat, emotionless voice. "Most of my memory is gone. But I know one thing for sure. You killed me."

"That's ridiculous," Melissa cried. "Tell me the truth. What are you doing here? Why are you trying to scare me with this ghost nonsense? How did you get in?"

"I'm dead," he said, turning around. His angry expression had softened. His eyes were watery. "I'm dead because you killed me."

His words chilled her. He wasn't joking.

But what he was saying was impossible. "You're as alive as I am!" she cried. She walked over to him, reached out, and grabbed his arm.

Her hand seemed to go right through him.

All she felt was a wisp of cold air.

"Oh, no!" she cried, covering her open mouth with her hand. She stepped back. Her heart was pounding now. She felt cold all over, chilled inside and out. She tried to scream but no sound came out.

He smiled, a grim smile. Her horrified reaction seemed to please him. "You believe me now."

"You're—you're a ghost." She wanted to run, but her legs were trembling. She felt weak all over. She slumped down onto the bed and stared up at him.

"Now you believe in ghosts," he said, his smile fading. "Isn't it amazing how a few seconds can change your life. Or *end* it?"

"But I *know* I didn't kill you," Melissa insisted. "It isn't something I'd forget, you know."

"You did." He pulled out the chair in front of her dressing table, turned it around, and sat down on it, leaning his chin against the seat back. "I can't remember how, but you killed me."

"Why? Why did I kill you?" Melissa asked.

He'd be good-looking if he washed his hair and stopped sneering like that, she thought.

"I don't remember," he said with some sadness.

"What's your name?"

"Paul."

"Paul what?"

"I don't remember."

"Huh? You don't remember your own last name?"

"I told you, I don't have much memory. Death screws you up in a lot of ways, you know. Oh, how would you know!" He slammed both hands against the chair back. They didn't make a sound. "I keep

53

fading in and out. I can't control it. I can hardly remember anything."

"If you have no memory, what makes you think I killed you? You're haunting the wrong house, Paul. And that's the truth."

He shook his head. "No. It's one of the few things I do know. You killed me, Melissa. I do know one other thing too."

"What?"

"I know why I've come back." He stood up and started toward her. "I've come back to pay you back. I've come back to kill *you!*"

"No!"

She jumped off the bed and started backing toward the bedroom door. He's crazy, she thought. Totally crazy. I've got to get away.

He stared into her eyes. "Scared, huh?"

"Yes," she admitted.

"Good. You should be. You finally got wise."

"I-I'll scream."

"You screamed before. It didn't do you much good. And it won't help much to run away either. You can't run from a ghost, Melissa. Haven't you seen any horror movies?"

"You're making a big mistake, Paul. I didn't kill you. Really."

She was only a few feet from the door. If she backed up a few more steps, she could be out of the room and down the steps.

But then what?

"You've got to believe me," she said. "I never knew

54

you! I've never seen you. I couldn't have been the one. It's all a big mistake."

He didn't say anything, just shook his head, staring coldly at her.

She realized she was shivering, shivering all over.

It was freezing cold in the room. The sudden cold last night. The sudden cold in the car. He brought the cold. He did it, she realized.

She backed up and bumped into the wall.

He moved quickly. Before she could get through the door, he was right in front of her. He raised his arms to block her path. His face was inches from hers.

He was so cold, so terribly, sickeningly cold.

"I didn't do it, Paul!" Her voice came out choked and small.

"You're a liar," he said quietly, and his handsome face suddenly turned quite ugly. "A rich liar. And rich liars have to die!"

chapter

8

"No, wait—" Melissa pleaded, raising her hands in front of her face as if to shield herself from him.

"Wait for what?"

Melissa thought frantically. What could she do to save her life? What could she do?

"Take your time," he said softly. "I'm not going anywhere."

She slowly lowered her hands. "Maybe I could help you somehow."

A bitter smile crossed his face.

"No. Really."

It was so cold. A damp, chilling cold. She wrapped her arms around herself, but it didn't help.

"I can help you. I can . . . uh . . . I can find the *real* person who killed you."

Where were her parents? Didn't they hear her

talking? Weren't they interested in whom she was talking to? If only one of them would come into her room, Paul would surely disappear the way he had in the past. And she'd be safe—at least for a little while.

"I already told you, Melissa," he said, making fun of her name as he said it. "I know who killed me. You did."

"But you're wrong. Besides . . ." She was thinking fast now, her mind jumping from thought to thought, trying to find some way, *any* way to stop this ghost from killing her. "Don't you want to find out how you died? Or why? Don't you want to know why?"

He looked away. He was thinking about what she said.

"I could help you," she added quickly, encouraged by his silence. "I *will* help you. I'll find out everything for you. I'll do everything I can to find the truth. Really."

He looked at her skeptically.

"Really," she repeated. "Really, I can help you. If you'll just give me a chance."

"Well . . ."

If only he'd back away. She was so cold, so freezing, shivering, shaking cold!

"Okay," he said. "There's no rush. I can kill you anytime I want."

He started to fade away, first his face and hands, then his jeans and denim jacket.

Then he was gone. And only the cold remained.

* * *

A few minutes later still trying to warm up, she backed her new car down the drive and headed to Buddy's house. It was a warm night, the temperature still in the seventies, but she closed the car windows and turned the heater way up.

She had stopped at the bottom of the stairs and considered telling her parents what had happened. But she quickly decided not to. They'd only think she had completely lost it. Even if they didn't think she had gone bananas, they would insist that she lie down or take some sleeping pills or they might even call a doctor. She really wanted to see Buddy. He was a lot more likely to listen to her than her mom and dad. He was a lot more likely to believe her.

She hoped.

Thinking about Paul, she drove through a red light. Luckily, there were no other cars nearby.

I've got to concentrate on driving, she warned herself.

But how could she?

She was being haunted by a ghost, a real ghost who had accused her of killing him. A ghost who had come back for revenge.

Where have I seen him before? Do I know him? Have I ever seen him?

She searched her memory, but came up empty.

No. No. No. I've never seen him in my life. I don't know *anyone* named Paul. I've never seen him around school. I don't remember any boy at Shadyside High being killed.

No. He's wrong. He's made a terrible mistake. And now what? What am I going to do about it?

She suddenly felt a shiver creep down her spine despite the scorching heat inside the car.

"Paul—are you here?" she asked aloud.

Silence.

"Paul—answer me. Are you here now?"

Silence.

No whispering of her name.

Complete silence.

She uttered a loud sigh, very relieved.

Then she thought: What if he *is* here but isn't answering?

A horn honked angrily. She looked back to see why, and realized she had gone through a four-way stop.

I shouldn't be driving, she thought.

She was almost to Buddy's house. He could drive them to the movies. But how could she go to the movies? She couldn't sit still. She couldn't concentrate on a movie. She had to *do* something.

Maybe Buddy would know what to do.

A few minutes later he met her at his front door. "Hi. Where've you been?" He looked at his watch.

"It's a long story," she said. "Aren't you going to invite me in?"

"We'll be late for the movie." He was wearing 501 jeans and a pressed button-down, blue workshirt. He pushed open the screen door and stepped onto the front stoop beside her.

"I don't want to go to the movie. I want to talk."

His brown eyes widened in surprise. He looked past her to the drive. "You got your car back. Can I drive it?"

"Yeah. Sure. But you weren't listening to me. I really want to talk."

"Well, there's a real mob scene here. My sister has some friends over, and my parents have company too." He took her arm. "Why don't we take a drive and talk?"

"Okay," she said. She finally felt warm again, but the terror of the scene in her bedroom lingered in her mind. She took Buddy's arm. "Okay. Let's go."

"Why don't we drive up to River Ridge?" he asked, a sly smile crossing his face.

She dropped his arm. "No. I mean it, Buddy. I really need to talk to you."

The smile disappeared immediately. "Is everything okay?"

"No," she told him.

"You mean it's about us? You want to talk about you and me?"

Trying not to get exasperated with him, she shook her head and didn't say anything. He's an okay guy, she thought. I really do care about him. But he sure can be self-centered sometimes.

He held open the passenger door and she slipped into the seat. It was still stifling hot inside the car. She turned off the heater as he walked around to the driver's side. They wouldn't be needing it now.

A few minutes later they were driving slowly along Canyon Road, passing ranch-style houses with neat, small lawns on both sides of them. "I don't know where to start," Melissa said, leaning her head on his shoulder.

"This car really handles great," he said. "What's the problem, Lissa?"

"Do you remember anyone named Paul at school? Someone named Paul who was killed?"

"Killed?" He turned his head to give her a confused look.

"Yeah. Killed. Paul something. I don't know his last name."

Buddy thought about it. "No. No one from school has been killed."

"I didn't think so."

"Well, who is this guy, anyway?"

"I don't know. But remember I told you I thought there was someone in my room and I screamed and then we couldn't find anyone?"

"Yeah. Of course I remember."

"Well . . ." She stopped. Would he laugh at her? Would he think she was nuts? Or would he believe her?

It was too late to back down now. She had to tell him and hope that she could convince him.

"Please don't say anything until I've told you the whole story, okay?"

Again he looked confused. He started to turn left on Park Drive.

"No. Don't go through town," she said, putting her hand on his arm. "Please. Turn right. Let's just drive out to the country where there are no distractions."

He obediently turned right. "Melissa, please—stop all this suspense. Just tell me what's the matter."

She told him the whole story, speaking rapidly as if it would be more believable, make more sense if she got it all out at once. She was out of breath by the time she told Buddy how she persuaded the ghost to let her help him, to let her live for a while.

They were outside of Shadyside now, out in farm country, dark and flat. Buddy pulled the car off the road onto the tall grass of the shoulder, but he didn't cut the engine.

He turned to her, leaned close to her, and put a warm arm around her shoulder. "Lissa—you're shaking!"

"I-I'm so scared, Buddy."

He didn't say anything. She looked up to find him staring at her.

"Well, say something. What do you think?" she asked impatiently.

The full moon was low over the flat farm fields. Its yellow light reflected off the shiny hood of the car. Thin wisps of gray blue clouds floated in front of it, and it suddenly grew darker.

"At first I thought you were joking," Buddy said, his hand gently squeezing her shoulder.

"I'm not," she said quickly.

"No. I see." He stared out through the windshield at where the moon had been before it had been blanketed by the clouds. He seemed to be thinking hard. Finally he said, "You really don't believe in ghosts, do you?"

62

Melissa thought she might cry. She took a deep breath and held it. She didn't want to cry in front of him. She didn't want to cry at all. "I knew you wouldn't believe me," she whispered, her face turned away from him.

"But do *you* believe it?" he asked. "Do you really believe a dead boy named Paul is haunting your room and wants to kill you? Don't *you* find that a little hard to believe?"

"Yes, I believe it, Buddy," she said angrily, taking his hand and lifting it off her shoulder. "I was there. It happened. It all happened. I believe it."

He took her hand, which was cold and wet. "Melissa, I'm really worried about you. I think we have to get you some help right away."

"You won't believe me?"

"How *can* I? It's not possible. It's just not possible."

"Okay," Melissa said, crossing her arms and facing forward. "Drive back to my house. Come on. Let's go. I'm going to prove to you that I'm telling the truth."

chapter

9

"The Volvo's gone. I guess my parents went out." Melissa found the key in her bag and opened the front door.

Buddy held the screen door, then followed her into the house. The hall light was on, but the rest of the house was dark. Melissa walked to the living room and flicked the light switch. "I hate a dark house," she said.

Buddy followed her into the room, looking uncomfortable, his hands shoved into his jeans pockets. Melissa hadn't said a word to him the entire drive home.

"Lissa, sit down," he said softly, gesturing to the overstuffed, upholstered couch by the bay window.

"No," she said, shaking her head. "Come on up to my room. I want you to meet Paul."

"But this is a waste of time," he said. "Please—sit down. Let's try to talk logically about this."

"I *am* talking logically," she snapped. "I'm going to prove it to you now."

"There's no such thing as ghosts," Buddy said, shaking his head. "Even on Fear Street."

"Fear Street has nothing to do with it," Melissa said.

"But the Fear Street Prowler does," Buddy said. "You've been so upset about those news stories. You haven't been thinking clearly—"

Suddenly they heard floorboards squeaking in the front hall. Footsteps.

Buddy looked at her, his eyes wide with surprise—and fear.

Who was approaching? Was it the prowler? Was it Melissa's ghost?

Melissa stared back at Buddy. Neither of them moved. The footsteps grew louder, accompanied by the squeaking floorboards.

They both turned to the living-room entranceway as Marta walked into the room. She was carrying a stack of freshly laundered bath towels. Her blond hair, normally pinned back in a bun with bobby pins, had come undone. "I thought I heard someone come in," she said.

"Hi, Marta. It's only us," Melissa said, looking at Buddy, who seemed very relieved.

"Your parents went to the Daltons'," Marta said. "I was just going to take these towels upstairs, then go to bed."

65

"We'll close everything up," Melissa said.

Marta disappeared. They listened to her climb the stairs.

"You can close your mouth now," Melissa told Buddy.

"I . . . she . . . I just wasn't expecting . . ." He laughed.

"You were expecting to see the ghost," Melissa said. "See? You *do* believe me."

His expression turned serious. "Lissa, please. Please stop talking about this ghost. Let's try to figure out what you *really* saw. You know, you might have dreamed the whole thing. It's possible, isn't it?"

"Aaggh!" she cried out, exasperated. "How could I have dreamed it? I was awake, wide-awake!"

"But maybe you were asleep and didn't realize—"

She picked up a throw pillow and angrily heaved it at him. "Just shut up, okay?"

He caught the pillow against his chest and dropped it to the floor. "Lissa—"

"Come on upstairs," she said, walking quickly from the room. "When you see the ghost with your own eyes, maybe you won't think I'm crazy, or too stupid to know when I'm awake and when I'm asleep."

"I didn't mean—" he started, but she was already heading up the front stairs. He followed behind, leaning on the smooth, polished banister.

They passed Marta, who was heading down the stairs to her room in the back. If Marta thought it strange that the two of them were heading for Melissa's bedroom, her face didn't indicate it. She said good night pleasantly and continued down the stairs.

Melissa hesitated at the door to her room. She looked back at Buddy, as if to make sure he was following her and not chickening out, then she stepped inside and clicked on the lamp.

The room had been straightened up. Marta must have put away the clothes Melissa had scattered around. She had even straightened the dressing table, stowing away all of the jars and tubes of blusher, lipstick, and eye makeup. The bed had been made, the covers turned down, ready for Melissa to go to sleep.

"Well, where is he?" Buddy asked, speaking loudly even though he was standing right next to Melissa.

"He's here. I'm sure of it," Melissa said, walking toward the window.

Buddy plopped down on the bed and lay back, his hands behind his head. "Hey—we're all alone up here," he said as if realizing it for the first time.

"No, we're not," Melissa said quietly. "Paul?" she called. "Paul, are you here?" She turned her head and looked around the room.

They both listened in silence. Outside they could hear a car drive past, its radio blaring loudly.

"Paul, I brought someone to meet you," Melissa said. "I brought someone else who can help you."

Silence.

She turned back to the bed to see if Buddy was laughing at her. If he was laughing, she vowed, she'd never speak to him again.

But Buddy did not look amused. He was staring at

67

her with concern, his face drawn in a frown of concentration. "Melissa, please, come here." He sat up and patted the bedspread beside him. "Sit down."

"Paul?" Melissa refused to give up. "Come on, Paul."

Silence. No sign of the ghost.

"I can tell he's here. It's so cold in the room," Melissa said with a shiver.

"Come over here. I'll warm you up." Buddy flashed her a grin and patted the bed again.

"Paul? Are you here, Paul?" Melissa couldn't hide the desperation from her voice. He *had* to show himself now. He *had* to. Or else Buddy would believe she really was crazy.

She sat down on the edge of the bed. Buddy put his arm around her gently. "Hey—you're freezing cold."

"Aren't you cold?" she asked. "Don't you feel it too?"

"Not really," he said, pulling her head down onto his shoulder. "It's a warm August night."

It felt good to snuggle against him. Melissa closed her eyes.

Buddy put both arms around her. He pressed his face against hers. "I keep thinking maybe this is a gag," he said softly. "Some kind of practical joke you're playing on me. Except that's really not like you."

"It's no joke," Melissa said, starting to feel angry again. Did Buddy really think she was doing all this just to put him on, just for a stupid joke?

"Paul—please! Where are you?" she called.

Buddy pulled her face down close to his and started to kiss her.

"No, Buddy." She pulled back. "I'm really not in the mood."

"Sshhh. Come on," he said. He kissed her again, pressing his mouth hard, harder against hers. He wrapped his arms around her tightly.

He felt so warm, so safe.

For a brief second she lost herself in the kiss.

Then she opened her eyes and looked up. There was Paul, standing over them, watching them kiss, his dark eyes flaring, his mouth twisted angrily.

As Melissa tried to pull away from Buddy's embrace, Paul uttered a deafening cry and, arms outstretched, lunged at Buddy.

chapter

10

Melissa screamed and fell back on the bed, trying to get out of the way.

Startled, Buddy jumped to his feet and stared down at her.

"Lissa, what's the matter with you?" he shouted.

Melissa stared up at Paul, who was right behind Buddy, his face distorted with anger.

"Why did you scream like that?" Buddy demanded. "Have you lost your mind entirely?"

"Buddy, there he is!" Melissa cried, still on her back on the bed, pointing at Paul.

"Huh?" Buddy turned around. He and Paul were face to face, but Buddy's confused expression didn't change.

"Don't you see him?" Melissa cried. "Didn't you hear him scream at you?"

Buddy turned back to her, looking very worried.

"Don't get up," he told her. "Just lie still. I'm going to call your parents."

"Buddy, what on earth—"

"Some boyfriend," Paul scoffed, now looking amused. *"I'd* never treat you like that."

"Paul, make him see you," Melissa pleaded, sitting up.

"No, please, lie still," Buddy urged her. "You're going to be okay. Really."

"I guess he can't see me," Paul said. He put his hand on Buddy's shoulder. Buddy didn't react. "He can't feel me, either." He punched Buddy hard in the back.

"Buddy—watch out!" Melissa screamed, too late.

But Buddy didn't feel a thing.

Paul looked very disappointed.

"Paul, leave him alone!" Melissa cried.

"I-I'll go get Marta," Buddy said, looking panicked. "Don't get up. We'll call your parents. We'll get you something to calm you down."

"Buddy, just listen to me. Stop acting so stupid."

"He can't help it," Paul said, sneering. "He is stupid."

Suddenly Paul started to fade away. First he became transparent. Melissa could see right through him. Then he was just a shadowy outline. Then he was gone, leaving behind a rush of cold air.

"Didn't you even feel that?" Melissa asked Buddy.

"Feel what?"

"That cold air."

Buddy turned around. "It's breezy out tonight. Look at the curtains."

"Buddy, I'm not crazy." She climbed to her feet and started pacing along the side of the bed.

"No, of course not," Buddy said. "But maybe you're having some kind of a breakdown or something."

"I don't get it," she said, stopping right in front of him. "Why can't you just trust me? Paul was right here, right behind you. He screamed at you. He punched you in the back. I'm not hallucinating. It's just that only I can see him."

"Lissa, calm down. This is real life. It isn't some stupid TV sitcom."

"Oh, I see. So now I'm crazy *and* stupid."

"I didn't say that." He put his hands on her shoulders. "Can't you see how worried I am about you?"

She backed away, out of his grasp. "Well, go worry about me at home," she said angrily.

"What?" He looked really hurt.

"You heard me. Go home. I can see that I have to figure out what to do about the ghost without any help from you."

"But I *do* want to get you help. First we have to tell your parents about this. Then we have to—"

"Go home, Buddy," she said wearily.

"I don't want to leave you like this. Where's the ghost? Where do you see him now? Show me."

"He faded away. Just go home. Please. I'm begging you."

He stood staring at her, trying to read her eyes,

trying to decide what to do. "Okay. I'll go. If you're sure you'll be okay."

"Yeah. Sure," she said. "I'm going straight to bed, okay?"

"Call me first thing in the morning?"

"Okay." She gave him a weak smile.

A few seconds later she heard the front door slam behind him. She sat down wearily on the bed and stared out the window. The clouds had drifted away, leaving the moon round and golden again.

"Thanks, Paul," she said aloud. "You just cost me a boyfriend."

He appeared at the side of the bed, a pleased look on his face. "So what's the big loss? You can just buy another one, right?"

"Why do you keep talking about how rich I am all the time?"

"I know you rich girls. You're all alike," he said bitterly. "If I were alive, you wouldn't even look at me."

"How do you know that?" Melissa asked.

"I know it. You rich people like to stick together. It makes it easier for you to stick up your noses at people like me." He turned and walked over to the window. Melissa could see the full moon shining right through his back.

"Buddy isn't rich," she said, wondering why she was bothering to defend herself to him. "His father works at the post office."

"Then what do you see in Buddy?" Paul asked,

73

turning around to face her. "It can't be his great personality." He laughed a dirty laugh.

"Oh, shut up!" Melissa cried wearily. "Why don't you just go away and leave me alone?"

"If you were my girl, I would've been nicer to you," Paul said, ignoring her plea. "But you never would've given someone like me the time of day."

Is he jealous? Melissa suddenly thought. Is that why he appeared and screamed like that when Buddy was kissing me?

"Go away—please!"

A shadow fell over his face. His entire body seemed to be swallowed up by it. Now he was nothing but a dark, shadowy outline of himself. "I knew you'd break your promise to help me," he said, lowering his voice until once again it sounded like the wind in the car.

"No, Paul. I—"

"I should just kill you now."

The words were a whisper, a whisper in her ear.

"You hit Buddy. He couldn't even feel it," Melissa said, thinking out loud. "How are you going to kill me?"

"I did that for your benefit," he said, staring at her menacingly. "I was just fooling around. Don't worry. I can make myself felt. I turned the steering wheel in your precious new car, didn't I? You felt me when I almost pushed you out the window. I managed to open your birthday presents for you."

"Why—why did you do that?"

74

"You don't listen, do you?" The shadow shifted and floated toward her. "I came back here to kill you. And I will. But not yet. First I want to have some fun. . . ."

Melissa thanked the librarian and carried the little roll of microfilm to the viewing booth. It was early Monday morning, and the library was empty except for a man with very thick glasses at a table in the front, leaning over a *Wall Street Journal*, and a shabby, unshaved man, in a filthy overcoat, snoring loudly in an armchair.

I've got to find out the truth about Paul, she thought. Her next thought made her shudder: My life depends on it.

Taking a seat in front of a viewer, she thought about Buddy. He really was ridiculous Saturday night, she thought, feeling her anger return. If he'd only just given me a chance instead of acting like I was some kind of raving lunatic. Buddy had let her down, she realized, at a time when she really needed him.

Trying to insert the roll of microfilm, she dropped it and it clattered across the floor. She slammed her hand angrily against the side of the machine, scooted her chair back, and went chasing after it. It rolled a few inches from the battered, laceless shoes of the sleeping man. Melissa picked it up carefully, trying not to wake him. But he abruptly stopped snoring, opened one bloodshot eye, raised a finger to his lips, and loudly said, "Sssshhhhhhh!"

Melissa picked up the cartridge and carried it back

to the viewer. A few seconds later she had managed to insert it and was scanning over editions of the Shadyside *Courier* for the past six months.

She figured that the death of a local teenager would be front-page news, so she carefully scanned every front page. Then, just to be on the safe side, she also checked the local news pages and the obituary page.

It took a long time. She was careful not to skip a single day of the entire six months. When she finally finished scanning the most recent paper, she closed her tired eyes and rested them for a few minutes.

Nothing. She had found nothing at all. No story about Paul's death. In fact, she hadn't found a story about a single teenager dying.

Maybe I didn't go back far enough, she thought. Paul said he thought he had died recently. But he really didn't remember anything about when it had happened.

Maybe he's been dead for years, she thought, yawning and stretching. She looked at her watch. It was nearly lunchtime. Had she really been staring into this machine for nearly three hours?

Tired and discouraged, she returned the microfilm, stepped past the armchair where the man was still snoring away, and headed out the door. The fresh air and bright sunlight felt so good!

She crossed the sidewalk to her car and was about to climb in when she saw a familiar face. "Della! Hi!"

"Got your car back, huh?" Della called, hurrying up to greet Melissa, a stack of books in her arm. She was wearing a green, sleeveless top and white tennis shorts. "How's it running?"

"Great. What are you doing here? I'm so happy to see you."

"Just returning some books," Della said. "Want to wait for me? I'll only be a sec."

Della returned a few minutes later empty-handed. "So what are *you* doing here?" she asked, shielding her eyes from the sun with her hand.

"It's a weird story," Melissa said, sighing. She wondered if Della would believe her. Yes. Della was such a good friend. She probably would. "Della, do you remember a boy about our age who died? His name was Paul something."

"Paul Something?" Della laughed. "I knew a Greg Something and a Mike Something. But Paul—"

"No. Seriously," Melissa said, leaning back against the shiny fender of her car.

"He died?" Della asked, thinking. "I can't think of anyone. Why?"

Melissa had a sudden thought. "You know, I bet he didn't go to Shadyside. He said he was poor and everything."

"You *talked* to him?" Della asked, confused.

"I'll bet he went to South," Melissa said, caught up in her own thoughts. She pulled absentmindedly at a thick lock of her hair. "Yeah. I'll bet he did."

"Well, my cousin Tracy goes to South," Della said. "The one with the teeth?"

"She had them fixed," Della said. "Want to see if she's home?"

77

"Sure," Melissa said. "Do you have anything you have to do right now?"

"Not really," Della replied. "Returning the library books was the highlight of my day."

"I know what you mean. I'm ready for school to start too," Melissa groaned.

They climbed into the new car. Della admired the leather seats and inhaled the new-car smell as Melissa pulled away from the curb and headed west. "Tracy lives in the Old Village," Della said. "I'll direct you."

A short while later Melissa was maneuvering the car through the narrow streets of the Old Village, where the early residents of Shadyside had settled, most of them in the 1920s when the mill opened and the first factories were built. They found Tracy in her small front yard, chasing after two little kids she was baby-sitting.

Tracy was short and thin and had spiked blond hair. She looked about ten or twelve, even though she was sixteen. She was wearing faded jean cutoffs and a Hard Rock Cafe T-shirt. "Hi!" she called, giving up on catching the two laughing kids.

Melissa followed Della up onto the freshly mowed lawn. "Hi, Tracy. You remember Melissa?"

"Yeah. Sure," Tracy said. "You're the one with the hair."

"And you're the one with the teeth," Melissa said, laughing.

"Not anymore," Tracy said, and flashed them both a wide, perfect smile.

"Melissa wanted to ask you about a boy who went to South," Della said.

"Well . . . *maybe* he went to South," Melissa said, bending over to pick up a tennis ball to throw back to the two kids.

"Well, I know most of the kids at South," Tracy said, and then added, "unfortunately."

"Come on, Tracy," Della said. "South isn't that bad."

"It's a pit," Tracy said, kicking at a tall weed. "But what's the point of complaining? I'm a senior this year. Then I'm *out* of here!"

"Tracy, do you remember anything about a boy from your school who died?" Melissa asked eagerly.

"Huh?"

"Either this year or last year. Was there a boy from South about our age who died?"

"Well, yeah. There was," Tracy said, wrinkling her forehead. "There was a boy who died just before school let out last spring."

chapter

11

"Now where did I put that old yearbook?" Tracy said, standing on tiptoe to reach the cluttered top shelf of her closet. She had deposited the two kids in the den with a Disney cartoon on the VCR. Then she led Melissa and Della up to her room so she could show them a picture of the boy who had died.

"Oh. Here it is. Look out!" she cried as a stack of old magazines came crashing down to the floor. Tracy waited for the dust to settle, then pulled down the South High *Mirror.* "As you can see, I'm a saver."

"Do you ever look at any of those old magazines?" Della asked, staring up at the stacks of them that reached nearly to the ceiling.

"No. Not really," Tracy said, rapidly flipping through the pages of the yearbook. "Good grief. Did we really look like that? Look at me. I look like Alvin the Chipmunk."

"No. You're cuter than Alvin," Della said, laughing.

"You say the nicest things. Oh. Here he is. He was a sophomore."

"The boy who died?" Melissa asked eagerly.

"Yeah. It's not a very good picture. He's standing in the back row. You can only see half his face." Tracy handed the open book to Melissa.

"Where is he? I don't see—"

"Right there," Tracy said, putting her finger on the picture. "The tall, blond guy. His name was Vince. Vince Alexander. Yeah. I remember now. He was a swimmer. All-state, I think. He was killed in a diving accident. His head hit the end of the diving board. Ugh. It was terrible."

Melissa stood staring at the picture of the smiling blond boy. Della put a hand gently on her shoulder. "Lissa, are you okay?"

Melissa silently closed the yearbook. "Yeah. Fine. It's just . . . he's not the boy."

"Who are you looking for?" Tracy asked, taking the book and tossing it back up on the closet shelf.

"A boy named Paul," Melissa said. "I don't really know if he went to South."

"Why are you trying to find out about him?" Della asked.

"I . . . uh . . . promised someone I would," Melissa said.

Della gave her a curious look, but Melissa was determined not to say anything more.

They said good-bye to Tracy, who had to hurry into the den to stop a fight about who got to choose which cartoon to watch next. A few minutes later Melissa dropped Della off at her house, then turned and headed toward her own house.

The late-afternoon sun was still high in the sky. The windshield seemed to light up as she drove toward the sun, the road bubbling in the heat. Shadows from the trees she passed danced on the shiny hood. It all seemed unreal. She had the feeling that she had left the road, floated up from the ground, and was driving high in the sky, on her way to the sun.

"Get real," she said aloud, forcing herself to sit up straighter. She pulled down the sun visor and gripped the wheel tighter as if tightening her grip on reality. She concentrated on the curving road, ignoring the glare of the sun and the darting shadows on the car.

I'm not cracking up. I'm *not*. The ghost is real, she told herself. Paul is real. He lived. He existed. And he died. I'm not hallucinating him. Sure, the stories about the Fear Street Prowler had me a little unhinged. Sure, I was a little jumpy, a little nervous because of them. That's only normal.

But if Paul was real, how come she hadn't been able to find out anything about him?

"Paul, are you here?" she asked out loud and waited for a reply.

"Paul?"

Silence.

Would she ever be able to go anywhere without

82

wondering if he was invisible at her side, waiting, watching her, planning to kill her.

"Paul?"

No. He wasn't there.

She pulled into her driveway and stepped out of the car. Shielding her eyes from the sun, she started toward the house. But stopped just outside the living-room window.

Someone was inside the house. Someone—just a shadow—was moving about the living room.

Looking at the porch, Melissa saw that the front door was wide open. Had someone broken the lock and barged right into the house? She backed away from the window and pressed herself against the shingled wall. Was it the Fear Street Prowler?

She crept back up to the corner of the window and peered inside. The sun glared off the glass, making it hard to see anything. But, yes—someone was in there, pacing back and forth, a moving shadow among still shadows.

Was it Paul?

Had he come downstairs? Was he waiting for her there, waiting for the news she didn't have, the information she was unable to find?

A prowler wouldn't pace back and forth, would he?

Of course not.

Melissa took a deep breath, walked quickly past the window, and headed into the house to see who it was.

chapter

12

"*B*uddy!"

He spun around, startled by her cry. "Hi."

She saw that his hair was wet and very curly. He must have just washed it. He was wearing a sleeveless blue T-shirt and very Hawaiian-looking baggy trunks.

"What are you doing here?" she asked, feeling very relieved, but remembering how angry she was at him.

"Uh . . . your mom let me in. Then she had to go shopping. How are you?"

"Okay."

"I came to apologize."

"Really?" She sat down on the back of the leather couch and crossed her arms. "You really don't have to—"

"No. I want to. I mean . . . well, I mean I'm sorry. That's all." He took a few steps toward her.

"Buddy, you still don't believe me about Paul," she said, tugging at the silver pendant on her neck.

"Lissa, please—let's not start up with that."

"But if you don't believe me, if you just think I'm crazy—"

"I don't think you're crazy," he protested, shoving his hands into the pockets of his trunks. "Listen, I had an idea. Let's just go out tonight and have some fun. What do you say?"

She looked at him doubtfully. "Fun?"

"Yeah. I'll pick you up about eight and we'll go to Red Heat."

"Well . . ."

"Come on, Lissa. You've always wanted to go there."

Melissa smiled and uncrossed her arms. Buddy really was trying to be nice. He hated loud, crowded dance clubs. He had always refused to take her to Red Heat in the past. Now here he was suggesting it.

"Okay. Great!" she said. She walked over to him, leaned forward, and gave him a quick kiss on the cheek. "You're forgiven."

He grinned back at her. "That was easy. Wow. What would you have done if I'd asked you out for dinner too?"

"Don't look at me like that," she replied. "I'm not that kind of girl."

Before it had become a teen dance club, Red Heat had been a farm equipment warehouse. From the outside, the long, tall building still looked like a warehouse. But all thoughts of farm machinery vanished as soon as they stepped onto the hangar-size dance floor.

The concrete floor, nearly a city block long, had been covered with long strips of fifties-colors linoleum, pinks and blacks, orange squares on pale green, aqua and maroon, all unmatched, all clashing. When the long rows of colored, flashing lights struck the dance floor from above, the floor seemed to come to life, seemed to dance right along with the dancers above it, and the warehouse became a different world.

The walls had all been painted red, although it was seldom bright enough to see their true color. The rafters above had also been painted red. The long juice bar and all of the other furnishings were red, in keeping with the name Red Heat. Giant black speakers, mounted at regular intervals from the rafters, blasted the music down to the floor, which reverberated from the booming sound and echoed the music right back up beyond the rafters, trapping the dancers in the middle, encircling them with the music, holding them as if in a powerful spell.

"I guess they call it Red Heat because it's eight hundred degrees in here!" Buddy shouted, perspiration dripping down his forehead.

"What?" Melissa, holding on to his shoulders, leaned closer to hear what he was saying over the roar of the music.

They had been dancing for nearly an hour. Melissa, wearing a sparkly midriff-length top and black Spandex bicycle shorts under a thigh-length purple skirt, felt great—dizzy and exhausted, as if she were moving in a fast-flowing stream, a stream of lights, and sound, and people. It felt so good not to think about anything, just to move mindlessly, almost machine-like, to the music.

She hadn't thought about the ghost once.

Paul.

Where was he, anyway?

She had called to him in her room after dinner. But he hadn't replied. And there was no sign of him, no cold wind, no hushed whisper, no shifting shadows across the carpet.

"I haven't seen the ghost all day," she told Buddy, thinking about her morning in the library.

"What?" He pulled her off the dance floor, toward the red neon-lit juice bar against the far wall. "I've got to get something to drink."

"Me too. A Coke or something." They were both breathing hard. She followed closely behind Buddy, the music pounding on all sides. Red and green lights played against their faces, making them look unreal, like Halloween characters.

"What did you say?" Buddy asked, still shouting to be heard.

"Just a Coke or something." She wiped her forehead with a tissue from the small bag belted around her waist.

"No. Before that." The line at the juice bar was long and moving slowly.

"I said I hadn't seen Paul all day."

"I thought we weren't going to talk about that," Buddy said sharply.

"I wasn't. I mean, I didn't." She grabbed his arm. "Listen, Buddy, it's hard not to think about him. He's threatened to kill me."

"What?"

"You heard me. I told you the whole story. He thinks I killed him and unless I find out who really did it, he's going to—"

"Melissa!" He shouted her name angrily and threw up his hands. "Stop—please!"

She let go of his arm. "I can't stop. I can't stop because it's real. It's happening to me, Buddy. And I can't stop thinking about it. You're just going to have to believe me, and—"

He pulled out of line, his face red, then green, then red again, looking very upset. "No. Stop. I can't believe it. I just can't. You're going to spoil the whole night, Lissa!"

"No, I'm not!" she screamed. "You already have!"

She turned and started to run, bumping into a surprised couple. "Hey—watch where you're going!"

But she was already past them, making her way quickly across the endless, crowded dance floor, bumping into couples who didn't seem to notice, surrounded by the throbbing music, her heart pounding along with it, running through the flashing colors. At the end of the dance floor, she turned back to see if Buddy was following her. She felt angry, disappointed —and relieved—when she couldn't see him.

"Hey, miss, if you're coming back in, get your hand stamped!" the purple-haired young man called to her in a high-pitched voice.

Melissa ignored him, pushed hard against the heavy glass door, and escaped into the night.

It was a warm night, but the air felt cold against her skin. Breathing noisily, she bolted down the three concrete stairs and kept running across the gravel walk toward the parking lot.

Where was she going?

She didn't know. She didn't even think about it.

She was so angry, so hurt.

Buddy just wanted her to be cheerful and happy and pretend everything was okay. He wasn't the least bit interested in her problem, in her *very real* problem.

Buddy really thought she was crazy.

Crazy!

As long as she kept it to herself, he was happy. He didn't care.

He didn't care what happened to her. As long as she shut up about it.

Well, how could she shut up about it?

She stumbled on the gravel, her sneakers sliding hard, but managed to catch her balance before falling.

Where was she?

Without realizing it, she had run halfway across the vast parking lot. She was surrounded by rows of cars. Pale, white spotlights at the top of poles that circled the lot provided the only light. Car shadows lay unmoving at her feet like dark, sleeping animals.

She turned back toward the club. She hadn't realized she had run so far.

The sound of laughter made her turn around.

Some boys were sitting on car hoods at the dark edge of the lot. There were four or five of them, some long haired, some with spiky flattops, wearing blue denim jeans and black leather or denim jackets. They were leaning back on the car hoods, laughing, joking around, tilting their heads back to suck down beers in cans wrapped in brown paper bags.

Their laughter was loud and cruel. They had obviously been drinking for quite a while.

I'll just turn around, Melissa thought. I'll head back toward the club. I don't think they've even noticed me yet.

She took two steps back, trying to hide in the shadows of the cars.

One of them called to her. "Hey—how you doin'?" He raised his brown paper bag in a salute and grinned.

"Don't go!" another one yelled. "Join the party!"

Melissa shook her head and started to back away.

Two of the boys, both sitting on the low hood of a yellow Camaro, got into a playful shoving match. "You ask her," one of them said.

"No. You ask her."

The one on the left gave his friend a hard shove, and the laughing boy, his beer can flying up in the air, toppled off the car and rolled across the gravel to Melissa's feet.

"Hey, fox—" he started.

Uncertain of what to do, Melissa looked down at his grinning face. And then her mouth dropped open in surprise.

Even in the dim, gray light in this darkest part of the parking lot, she recognized him at once.

"Paul—what are you *doing* here?" she asked.

chapter

13

*H*e stared up at her. He didn't make any attempt to get up from the gravel. The wide, foolish grin seemed to be plastered to his face.

"Hey—do I know you?" he asked.

His friends laughed as if he had just cracked a very clever joke.

"Paul—" she started, her heart pounding, her throat suddenly dry.

"That's my name. Don't wear it out."

Again, laughter and knee slapping from his friends.

One of them walked over, a similar foolish grin on his face, bent down, and with great effort pulled Paul to his feet. The two of them stood unsteadily, staring at Melissa, looking her up and down.

Melissa was so startled to see Paul there in that dark parking lot with his loud, drunken friends that she forgot her fear. "You—you can see him?" she asked the boy who had pulled Paul to his feet.

They all laughed again.

Looking beyond Paul, she saw that they had all climbed down from the car hoods and were approaching her slowly, sipping from their brown paper bags as they walked.

"You really can see him?" Melissa repeated.

"Not if I see him first!" Paul cracked and dropped back down to his knees, laughing. It was obvious that he'd had too much to drink.

"But . . . you're real!" Melissa stammered.

This got a big reaction from all of them. They hooted and howled. Turning quickly, Melissa saw that they had formed a circle around her.

I'm trapped, she thought, feeling a rush of panic.

They're closing in on me.

"Yeah, I'm real," Paul said quietly, turning serious. "Want me to prove it?" He grabbed her arm.

"Let go of me!" Melissa shouted, forcing herself to sound more angry than afraid.

To her surprise, he quickly let go. "Hey—*you* were coming on to *me,* weren't you?" he said accusingly.

"No. I wasn't," Melissa protested, trying to figure out how to get away from these boys and get back to Buddy inside the club.

Why hadn't Buddy come looking for her? Didn't he care at all?

"You're just a tease, huh?" Paul said, sneering.

"Paul, why are you doing this?" she asked. "Why are you acting so . . . different?"

93

He glared at her. "Huh?"

"Yeah, Paul. Why are you acting so different?" One of Paul's friends, a boy with straight black hair down to his collar, mimicked Melissa. The boy stepped forward and grabbed Melissa's shoulder. "What do you see in him, anyway?"

"Hey—leave her alone," Paul said, his face suddenly turning ugly. He gave his friend a hard shove. The boy fell back against a new Oldsmobile. "She wants me—not you," Paul said.

The boy got up quickly. "Oh, yeah? How about we let *her* decide, okay?"

"She's already decided," Paul said, his hands curling into tight fists at his sides. His friend glared back at him, trying to decide whether to fight Paul or not.

"Stop it! Just stop it!" Melissa shouted, frightened and confused. How come his friends could see Paul so clearly? Was it possible that he wasn't a ghost after all? That he had somehow managed to trick her back in her room?

"Let me go!" she shouted and turned toward the club.

Paul laughed. "What's your hurry? Didn't you come out to play?"

She ignored him and took a few steps, her sneakers crunching on the gravel.

Two of Paul's friends moved to block her path.

She moved quickly to the right. They moved to the right. She started to the left. Grinning at each other, they moved left to block her once again.

94

"What's the matter?" Paul called after her. "You too good for us?"

"I want to go now," Melissa said slowly, determinedly, pronouncing each word distinctly. She didn't want them to know how frightened she was. Her knees were shaking and her voice had a slight quiver.

"Let her go," the boy Paul had shoved said quietly.

"Don't tell me what to do!" Paul screamed, turning on his friend. "Don't ever tell me what to do!"

"I just said, let her go," the boy replied, standing his ground.

"I'll let her go when I'm finished with her," Paul said, his voice turning low and threatening. And without any further warning, he lunged at his friend, grabbing his shoulders, and the two of them fell to the gravel, rolling around, wrestling hard and furiously, screaming and cursing at each other as the others gleefully looked on.

Melissa hesitated for only a second, then began running back across the parking lot toward the club. She had gone only a few steps when they realized she was escaping.

"Hey—come back here!"

She recognized Paul's angry voice and kept running. The rows of cars on both sides of her seemed endless. The gravel flew from under her sneakers.

She heard them coming after her, tried to pick up speed, slipping and sliding, and nearly lost her balance. The lights were out in that section of the parking

95

lot, and the sudden darkness frightened her even more.

They're catching up, she realized. What are they going to do to me?

"Hey, Blondie, we just want to have some fun!" one of them yelled. The others laughed and kept chasing her.

Several couples were watching them in the parking lot. Because of all the laughter, they must have thought it was all a joke. The double glass-door entrance to the club came into view. Melissa gasped for breath. Her head throbbed and her chest felt as if it were about to explode.

Would she be safe inside the club? Yes. They wouldn't follow her in there.

"Hey, Blondie, we won't hurt you! Honest!"

Why did Paul act so weird, so cold, so horrible? She had spent most of the day trying to help him, trying to find out what really happened to him. Now here he was, acting so gross, like a complete animal, as if he didn't know her at all. Was he just showing off for his buddies?

Two couples came out of the club and stood in front of the entrance, talking and giggling. "Help!" Melissa tried to call to them, but her cry was strangled in her throat. She was too out of breath to make a sound.

"Help me, please!" She tried again, and again the words came out weak, a soundless groan. The two couples laughed among themselves and didn't turn around.

She stepped into the glare from the flashing red spotlight, the light pulsating on and off as quickly as her heartbeat. I'm almost there, she thought, and turning back she saw that Paul and his friends were no longer chasing her.

In fact, they were gone.

Shadows slid through the long aisle of cars. Was that them? Were they running off? Were they hiding out there, waiting for her to return?

When did they stop chasing her? And where did they go?

She held her hand over her eyes, trying to keep out the blinding, flashing red light. The club doors opened and music burst out into the silence, startling her.

The doors shut. The parking lot fell silent once again.

Still shielding her eyes, Melissa stared out at the rows of cars. Where did Paul and his friends go? How did they disappear so quickly?

Were they *all* ghosts?

"Hey, Melissa!"

Lost in her thoughts, still trying to calm her pounding heart, she didn't hear the voice.

"Melissa!"

A hand touched her shoulder.

"No!" she screamed and backed away.

"What's wrong?" Buddy asked, looking surprised and concerned, flashing red, then black, then red again under the spotlight.

"Buddy, please, take me home," she said. She grabbed his arm. He felt so solid, so real.

97

"I couldn't find you," he said. "I didn't know you were outside."

"I'm sorry—" she started. She heard a noise, a scuffling sound, somewhere down the nearest row of cars. Was that Paul and his friends?

Buddy followed her gaze. "Melissa, what is it?"

"I—I thought I saw something."

"I don't see anything. It's so dark down there. Some of the lights are out."

She held on to him tightly. They were both flashing red, then black, red, then black, as if they were materializing and then disappearing like ghosts.

"You want to go home?"

"Yes. Thanks."

"Melissa, you're shaking all over."

"I'm just . . . tired, I guess." She wasn't going to tell him that she saw Paul in the parking lot. Paul and his ghost friends. Paul and his real friends. She knew if she told Buddy, they'd just start to argue again. He'd get that worried look on his face and say they should tell her parents immediately.

She couldn't tell him. She knew she couldn't. It would just make him more certain that she was losing it, cracking up. Then her parents would get into the act, and her life would get even more complicated than it already was.

"Sorry I'm such a downer," she said. "Please take me home."

He put his arm around her shoulders and led her to the car. Melissa walked quickly, alert to any sound or sign that Paul and his friends were there, hiding, watching, waiting.

They had disappeared. Disappeared into thin air.

She slid into the passenger seat and closed her eyes. Even with her eyelids shut tight, the flashing red light didn't go away.

Buddy talked excitedly about what a great club Red Heat was, and what a great sound system they had, and how they should go there more often, but what a shame it was that the club was so expensive. He had obviously decided to forget the fact that they had had an argument and that Melissa had stormed out of the club.

Melissa had to struggle to remember what the argument had been about. Paul. Of course, it was about Paul.

Maybe Buddy figured if he ignored the whole thing, Paul would just go away.

Melissa wished Buddy was right.

If only Paul *would* go away . .

An hour later, in bed, Melissa couldn't get to sleep. When she closed her eyes, she saw Paul and his friends, saw them shoving one another against the cars, tilting their heads back to drink from the brown paper bags, saw them circling her, closing in on her.

She couldn't get Paul's face out of her mind, his cruel laughter, the way he threatened her, the way he grabbed her so fiercely, the way he looked at her.

The way he hated her.

Yes. That was what Melissa found so frightening.

Paul *hated* her.

She didn't even know him, and he hated her.

It was a warm, humid night, but she pulled the covers up to her chin. The bedroom window was closed and locked. The streetlight down below cast a pale yellow light onto the ceiling.

I've never been hated before, Melissa thought.

Sure, there had been kids who didn't like her very much, kids she didn't get along with. But she had never been hated so blindly, so heatedly. Never.

He really has come back to kill me, she thought.

Somehow she had never taken his threat seriously. She had thought she could reason with him, talk to him, help him. He had seemed jealous of Buddy, after all. And because of that, Melissa had even fooled herself into thinking that maybe Paul wasn't so bad after all.

But seeing him there on that dark parking lot with his friends, seeing how he fought them, how hard he was, how bitter, how cruel, she realized that she was wrong about him.

He would never be her friend.

He could kill her. He meant what he said.

He hated her that much.

She sat straight up when she felt the rush of cold air. A few seconds later Paul appeared, first a dark outline in front of the window, then a shadowy form moving quickly to the foot of the bed.

Melissa couldn't see his face. It was covered in

shadow. She saw that he was still wearing the straight-legged blue denim jeans and the faded denim jacket.

He started to move closer.

"Get out of here!" she screamed, gripping the covers. "Stay away from me! Leave me alone!"

The ghost seemed to float up until he was looming above her, glowing dark eyes staring coldly down at her.

"Get out!" Melissa repeated, feeling his eyes burn into hers. "Just go away!"

The ghost began to fade. The eyes dimmed, the face darkened, the floating form became a dim outline, shades of gray against the pale light from the street.

"I'll be back. I'm not finished here," Paul said, words more chilling than the air he left behind.

chapter

_____

14

"No, I can't, Della. Not this morning anyway."

Melissa pulled back the curtain and looked out the bedroom window. It was a gray day, heavy, dark clouds covering the sky. She shifted the phone from one ear to the other.

"Yeah. Buddy and I had a pretty good time last night." She didn't feel like getting into it with Della first thing in the morning. She realized she hadn't confided at all in her best friend. She wanted to tell her about Paul. She *needed* to. Della would probably believe her, and Melissa desperately needed someone to believe her.

I'll tell her all about it when my parents are away, when I stay at her house this weekend, Melissa thought.

They chatted aimlessly for a few more minutes. Then Melissa promised to call her later, hung up, and went down to breakfast.

She found her mother, wearing a maroon running suit, at the table, with the morning paper and a half-eaten dry English muffin. Her father, leaning on the kitchen counter, was having a heated telephone discussion with someone about plane reservations.

"Morning," Mrs. Dryden muttered from behind her paper.

"Who's Daddy talking to?" Melissa asked, pouring herself a bowl of corn flakes.

"Travel agent," her mother said, chewing the dry, toasted muffin. "Some problem with our tickets to Las Vegas. He's going in late today." She lowered the paper and stared at Melissa. "Look at the rings under your eyes."

Melissa put down the milk carton. "Mother, that's physically impossible. You can't look at your own eyes."

"Didn't you sleep?"

"Not too well," Melissa admitted.

"That sweatshirt is wrinkled," her mother said, folding the newspaper.

"I know. I'm a slob."

"Didn't it used to be white?"

"No, Mother, it was always gray." Melissa made a face.

"I'm not interested in your problems." Mr. Dryden's voice boomed into the phone. "You have to

103

get us boarding passes with our tickets. I'm not taking the chance of being bumped from the plane. I know how airlines overbook these days."

"Poor Daddy," Melissa said, with a mouth full of corn flakes.

"I really think you should change your mind," her mother said.

"What?"

"You know. Come to the convention with us. It'll do you good to get away. You've had such a boring summer."

Melissa laughed. "Believe me, Mother, it hasn't been boring."

Her mother looked disappointed. "You won't come?"

"No. Really. I don't think so."

Melissa pretended to concentrate on her corn flakes. Running away to Las Vegas, she knew, wouldn't help her. She had to find out the truth about Paul, find out what really happened to him. It was the only way she could get rid of him, the only way he would leave her alone.

Melissa ate quickly, pushed her chair away from the table, and waving to her father, headed toward the front door. "Where are you off to?" Mrs. Dryden called after her.

"Just meeting Della," Melissa lied.

"Looks like rain," her mother said.

"I won't melt."

The sky looked a little less threatening as she backed her car down the drive. The clouds had lifted.

They looked as if they might blow past without leaving any rain. Melissa turned down The Mill Road and headed toward town. The dashboard clock read 11:58. How had she slept so late?

She turned into the large Shop 'N' Stop parking lot on Division Street and slowly cruised the rows of cars looking for a parking place. Maybe today won't be a total waste of time like yesterday, she thought. Maybe today I'll find some answers about Paul.

Melissa had recognized one of the boys with Paul in the parking lot the night before. His name was Frankie. She couldn't remember his last name. She'd thought he looked familiar, but she didn't remember who he was until it came to her in the middle of the night. He delivered groceries for the Shop 'N' Stop.

The parking lot was completely full, so Melissa had to park on the street outside the lot. She climbed out, locked the car, and crossed the lot, walking quickly, starting to feel nervous.

Frankie, she had noticed, had hung back the night before. He hadn't threatened her or stood in her way. In fact, he had seemed a little embarrassed by the whole incident.

Or maybe that was just wishful thinking on Melissa's part.

Anyway, she told herself, talking to him while he's at work is perfectly safe. He's not going to try anything in the middle of the supermarket.

Frankie was her only clue now, the only person she knew who actually could tell her about Paul, who maybe could clear everything up for her.

I hope he's here today. I hope I can find him. . . .

The electric doors swung open with a loud buzz, and Melissa stepped into the frigid air of the vast supermarket, with its clattering shopping carts and rhythmic beeping of computerized cash registers.

She walked through the produce department, past a tall display of some new kind of cherry soda. She was surprised to see Frankie without having to search for him. He was at the end of the nearest checkout line, bagging groceries for a young woman with a baby in a carrier on her back.

Melissa hesitated, wondering what she was going to say to him. Maybe this is a stupid idea, she thought.

Frankie looked up, having packed the last of the groceries, and saw her. At first he seemed confused, as if he didn't remember who she was. Then suddenly a broad smile of recognition spread over his face.

As Melissa walked up to him, the smile faded, replaced by a wary look. "Frankie?" she asked uncertainly.

"Hey, look—I don't want no trouble," he said, waving her away. His straight brown hair was tied behind his head in a short ponytail. He was wearing a long white Shop 'N' Stop apron over black jeans and a crisp blue work shirt.

"No, I—" Melissa started.

"I didn't do nothing last night. The other guys— I didn't think they should've . . ." His voice trailed off. He was looking past Melissa to a large woman behind a counter, probably his supervisor.

"I didn't come because of last night. I want to ask you about something else."

He shook his head, straightened the stack of brown grocery bags.

"It'll only take a minute. I promise," Melissa pleaded.

He hesitated. "Well, okay. I'll take my break now." He walked over and said something to the woman behind the counter, then motioned for Melissa to follow him.

She followed him down the long produce aisle to a large storeroom against the back wall. It was even colder in this room and smelled of rotting fruits and vegetables.

Frankie pulled down a wooden crate and motioned for her to sit down. Melissa lowered herself onto the crate and crossed her legs. He continued to stand. "I only get ten minutes for my break," he said, waving to two guys unloading lettuce from big crates into a shopping cart.

"I want to ask you about Paul," Melissa said, unsure of how to start.

Frankie smiled. "You really got the hots for Paul, huh?"

Melissa could feel herself blushing. "No. That's not why . . . I mean . . . Listen, you and Paul were friends?"

"Yeah. We're buddies. Paul's a pretty bad dude."

"What do you mean by bad?" she asked uncomfortably, suddenly feeling very stupid, wishing she hadn't come here.

Frankie shrugged. "He's just bad, that's all." His face filled with suspicion. "Hey, listen—if Paul did something wrong . . . or something, I don't know anything about it."

"No, listen, I—"

"I mean, he's my buddy, but I don't go along with some things. I mean, I don't know anything at all. Really."

Frankie looked up at the clock above the storeroom door. Melissa realized this wasn't going well at all. She decided she'd better get to the point. "When did Paul die?" she asked.

Frankie's mouth dropped open. He pulled at his ponytail. "Huh?"

"Paul. You know. When did he die? Can you tell me—"

"Paul's dead?" He sat down on the floor next to Melissa. "When? Last night? No. No. Wait. That's impossible. I talked to him on the phone this morning. Before work."

Now Melissa was completely confused. "Maybe we're talking about different Pauls," she said.

"Yeah. Maybe." Frankie still looked very upset.

"The Paul I'm talking about died some time ago," Melissa said.

Frankie got to his feet slowly. "Hey—you really scared me."

"I-I'm sorry," Melissa stammered. "But I wanted to ask you—"

Frankie looked up at the clock again. "Hey, sorry, but I gotta get back to work and I need a soda first. If

I'm late after a break, I'll be busted." He turned and hurried from the storeroom.

The swinging doors closed behind him. Melissa sat on the crate for a few minutes, staring at the stack of crates against the wall, trying to make sense of what he had just told her.

It didn't make sense.

They were talking about the same Paul. That was the only thing Melissa was certain of. But was Paul dead or alive, a living, breathing human or a ghost?

She knew that Paul was a ghost. He had told her he was a ghost. He appeared and disappeared like a ghost.

So how could Frankie not realize that his buddy was dead? How could he have talked to Paul before going to work?

Melissa stood up and walked slowly out of the storeroom, feeling as disappointed as she was confused. Frankie had been her one clue, her one hope. But he had only helped to make things more baffling than ever.

As she walked past him to the exit, Frankie looked up from the bag he was packing and gave her a curious look.

He thinks I'm crazy, Melissa thought.

Maybe I am.

Stepping outside the supermarket, she saw that the pavement was wet. It must have rained while she was inside, and now the sky was clearing, sunlight sparkling off the wet cars in the parking lot.

She walked around a large puddle and headed for her car. Thinking about Frankie, she didn't see the car backing out of its space until it nearly hit her.

"Watch where you're going!" a woman's voice yelled.

Melissa dodged away, shocked to alertness, and stepped into a puddle, cold water splashing over her sneakers. I've got to pay attention, she thought, making her way down the endless rows of cars to the street.

She heard footsteps behind her, but didn't think anything of them. A car trunk slammed shut. A baby was crying back by the supermarket.

She heard the footsteps again as she turned a corner and headed down the last row of cars. They sounded closer behind her now. She turned around, just to see who it was—and saw a flash of color as someone ducked behind a car.

What's going on? she wondered.

Was she seeing things?

She turned and started walking again, a little faster.

She took several steps, then spun around again.

Again, a flash of dark color. A dark blue jacket maybe. Dark hair. Whoever it was disappeared behind a blue Toyota.

Someone's following me. That was her first thought.

It looks like Paul. That was her second.

But why would Paul hide behind a car? He could appear and disappear. He didn't have to hide.

Should she stop and wait him out?

No. She could feel the fear creeping up her body, catching at her throat. No. She decided to run.

She turned and, ignoring the puddles, began running to the street. He isn't following me—is he? No, he isn't. He can't be.

Yes.

The footsteps, scraping against the pavement, splashing through the puddles. Right behind her now. Closer. Running faster than she was.

What was the point of running? She stopped and turned. "Paul!"

He stepped close and grabbed her shoulder.

chapter
15

"**P**aul!"

He grinned at her, a hard, cold grin, not friendly, not amused. His hand tightened on her shoulder.

"Paul, why—"

"You missed me, huh?"

"What? What do you mean?"

"I heard you calling me back there."

"Let go, Paul. You're hurting me."

He eased his grip but didn't release her.

"I thought I saw you following me, so I called you. Let go of me."

He slowly let go. He was standing close to her, too close. He pressed his face close to her cheek. She could feel his breath, hot against her skin.

Feel his breath?

Did a ghost breathe?

Frightened, she took a step back, but he moved forward, staying with her.

"Why'd you run away last night?" he asked, his dark, cold eyes staring into hers. "You and me could have a good thing going."

"You were so awful," she said. "And those disgusting friends of yours."

"Hey—they're my buddies." He seemed amused by her reaction to them. "They're good guys."

"What do you want, Paul?" She took another step back and realized she had backed into the trunk of a big Oldsmobile. He moved forward, blocking her escape. If he took one more step, she'd be pinned against the trunk.

"What do I want?" He laughed. "What does any red-blooded American boy want from a nice-looking girl?"

"Get away from me. Let me go. Why are you acting like this?"

He looked hurt. "Hey, listen, *you* came on to *me* last night."

"I did not."

"Looked that way to me."

"I don't understand. Why are you acting like such a creep? I've been trying to help you."

"Huh?"

"Like I promised."

"Huh?" He looked confused. He scratched the side of his face, then unbuttoned his denim jacket, revealing a blue, sleeveless T-shirt underneath. "You want to help me?" He gave her a dirty grin.

She shoved him and pulled away from the trunk, running hard between cars to get to her car on the street.

"Hey—" he called, trotting after her. "Don't run away again. I thought you wanted to help me."

"Just go away!" she shouted.

"Now you're hurting my feelings," he called, several yards behind her. "I don't like that. I don't like it when rich, snobby girls hurt my feelings."

He's crazy, she thought. I've got to get away from him. She reached her car, pulled the door handle. It didn't budge. She forgot she had locked it.

She plunged her hand into her bag and began frantically rummaging around for her keys. But now he had caught up to her. Smiling triumphantly, he grabbed her bag and held it out of her reach.

"Give it back," she demanded, reaching for it and missing.

He backed up, laughing, still holding her bag high above his head.

"Give it back, Paul."

He laughed again. "Come and get it!"

"Paul!" She grabbed for it, but he twirled away, keeping it out of her reach. "Give it back—now! You're not funny!"

He didn't give back the bag, and his smile faded. "You're not gonna give me a chance, are you?" he said.

"What?"

"You heard me."

"I don't know what you're talking about. Just give me back my bag."

"I'm not a bad guy. Really. But you'd never want to find that out."

"Paul, you're talking crazy. Please give me back my bag. I've got to go." She made another wild grab for the bag. He pulled it out of her reach and drew it under his arm.

"I can play rough," he said, his dark eyes wild as they stared into hers. "I can play real rough if I have to."

"Paul—come on!" she cried.

"How did you know my name?" he demanded.

"What? You told it to me."

"I never did. Come on. Tell me. Where'd you learn my name?"

"Paul, don't be ridiculous—"

She saw the police car before he did. The black-and-white car, cruising slowly, pulled up beside her car. The officer on the passenger side poked his head out the window. "Problem here?"

"No. No problem," Melissa answered quickly as Paul handed her back her bag. She expected him to disappear into thin air, but he stood there frozen on the spot, staring at the policeman, a phony-looking smile on his face.

"Well, I think there is a problem," the policeman said.

He turned and said something to his partner behind the wheel. Then he opened the door and, eyeing Melissa and Paul, slowly stepped out of the police car.

"This your car?" he asked Melissa.

She nodded, glancing at Paul, who was standing with his hands behind his back, looking very pale and worried.

"Well, it's in a No Parking zone." He pointed to a tall sign several yards away. "You're supposed to park inside the lot, not outside. What's your name? Can I see your driver's license?"

"Melissa Dryden," she said searching in her bag for her wallet. "I didn't see the sign. I didn't realize . . ." She pulled out her driver's license and handed it to him.

He started to examine it when his partner leaned out of the car and shouted, "Forget it, Ernie. We've got an emergency call. Let's roll!"

The blaring siren starting up made Melissa jump.

"Sorry, miss." The policeman tossed the license to her and jumped back into his car. She watched them roar off.

"Hey, listen—" Paul said, smiling and acting very relieved. "You got a break there, huh? I'd never get a break like that. That's for sure."

"Bye," she said, unlocking the car and sliding behind the wheel.

"Whoa. Wait, Melissa, I—uh—I'm sorry I gave you a hard time," he said, looking contrite. "I was just having a little fun. I didn't mean—"

She slammed the car door and missed the rest of what he had to say. The car started right up, and a few seconds later she pulled away, leaving him on the curb, staring after her, an unhappy expression on his face.

She watched him in the rearview mirror, expecting him to disappear into thin air. But he didn't move.

I've got to get rid of him, she thought, speeding through a yellow light, then making a sharp left turn. He's following me everywhere. He's taking over my life.

And he wants to hurt me.

A few minutes later she parked the car in the drive, ran into the house, shouted hello to Marta, who was vacuuming the living room, and ran up to her room.

"No!" she shouted.

Paul, sitting on her bed, stood up quickly.

"No! Leave me alone! Stop following me! Just leave me alone!"

Ignoring her pleas, he moved toward her quickly, his dark eyes aglow.

chapter
16

*S*he stepped back toward the hallway. He stopped in the center of the room. The strong sunlight from the bedroom window seemed to shine right through him. His dark hair, his denim jacket, his jeans were all outlined in gold.

"Hey, what's happening?" he asked.

Melissa didn't reply. She stood waiting to see if he'd come closer.

"Why are you so scared of me all of a sudden?" he asked, looking suspicious.

"Don't play dumb," Melissa said, her arms crossed protectively in front of her.

"I'm losing control," he said softly, and as he spoke his entire body shimmered and started to fade, making the sunlight from the window seem brighter. "I can't seem to control my strength. I keep fading in and out."

"You were solid enough in the parking lot," Melissa said angrily.

"Huh?" The shimmering slowly stopped and he stood solidly on the carpet once again. He scratched the side of his jaw. For the first time, Melissa realized, he looked frightened. Behind the anger and bitterness, he was just a frightened teenager.

"How'd you get back here so quickly?" Melissa asked. The sunlight was hurting her eyes, making it hard to see him. She circled around him, keeping her distance, and sat down on the windowsill, her back to the sun.

"Get back? What are you talking about? Are you playing some kind of mind game on me?"

"I left you standing outside the parking lot. Now here you are," she said. The sun felt good on her back.

He shook his head and started to pace. "You've totally lost it."

"You've totally lost it," Melissa told him. "Not me. You're not going to tell me that—"

"I've been here all morning," he said. "Sort of drifting in and out."

Melissa pushed herself off the windowsill and stood up. "Come on, Paul, you were at the supermarket."

He shook his head. "No. It wasn't me."

"You grabbed my bag and wouldn't give it back."

He moved his hand up to her desk lamp. His hand went through the lamp. "I can't grab anything today," he said with real sadness. "I couldn't grab your bag if I wanted to." His whole body seemed to fade, as if the effort of talking was too much for him.

"I don't believe you," Melissa said. "You're playing some kind of trick."

He didn't reply, just stared back at her, trying to read her face, trying to read her thoughts.

What's he doing? Melissa asked herself. Is he pretending to be weak? He looks so sad, so frightened now. Is he just trying to throw me off guard for some reason? Just trying to confuse me?

"I suppose it wasn't you last night," she said.

He looked surprised. "Last night? When I appeared here last night, you screamed at me like a nut and told me to leave you alone."

"No, I meant before that," Melissa said impatiently. "At the dance club."

"Dance club?" He snickered. "That wasn't me either." He floated down to the carpet, seemed to sink into it, his whole body disappearing, then resurfacing on top of it. "Someone who looked like me, maybe."

She refused to believe him. "It was you, Paul. It wasn't a look-alike. You mean you don't remember?"

"I remember last night. I went out, trying to find my old neighborhood. But I couldn't find it, couldn't remember where it was. So I came back here."

"You're putting me on, right? You were with your buddies, sitting on cars, drinking beers, and when I came out, you—"

"My buddies? What buddies?"

"I don't know their names. Frankie was one of them. And the rest, I don't know."

"Frankie?" A smile slowly crossed his face, a smile of recognition. "Yeah. Frankie. Hey—I remember him. Frankie Marcuso. Yeah. He was my neighbor. Great guy. Wow. I'd forgotten all about him. Who else was there?"

His whole face brightened when I mentioned his friend, Melissa thought. I've been so scared of him, too scared to realize how lonely and frightened he is.

"I don't know," Melissa replied, her mind whirling. "I don't know your friends. They were creeps."

"Hey, wait a minute." He floated to his feet. "Don't put my buddies down."

"Listen, is this some kind of joke or something?" Melissa asked, leaning back against the windowsill. "Are you putting me on?"

"No. No joke," he said quietly, looking away from her.

"Then we have to figure this out," Melissa said, supporting her chin with both hands. "Don't you see? You weren't there last night and this morning. But you *were* there."

"Huh?"

"You were in two places at once, Paul. Right?"

She waited for him to think about it. He looked very confused, pacing rapidly back and forth the length of her bedroom. "Yeah. I guess so. I was in two places at once. So what does it mean?"

Melissa looked down at the floor, thinking hard. The Paul at the dance club and at the parking lot had seemed so different, so much more solid, so much angrier, tougher, so much more—alive!

Alive!

121

She stared at the ghost, floating so lightly, so soundlessly back and forth across the carpet. And she had an idea.

"Paul, I think I know."

He stopped pacing. "I think I know too." He stared at her angrily. "This is all a trick, isn't it? Some kind of stupid trick to stall for time."

"No. Stop. That isn't it—"

"I should've known," he muttered to himself, turning his back on her.

"Paul, just listen to me. I think maybe I've figured out what's happening."

He didn't turn around.

She decided to say it anyway. "We just assumed you were a ghost from the past," she said.

"Huh? What do you mean?" he asked without turning around.

"We assumed that you died some time ago. You died in the past, and you've come from the past to the present to avenge your death."

"Yeah, well . . . of course," he said, obviously confused, not understanding where her thoughts were leading. He turned around and looked at her skeptically, waiting to see what came next.

"Well, maybe we were wrong," Melissa said, struggling to get her idea straight in her own mind. "What if you are a ghost from the future?"

"What? You mean like some stupid science-fiction movie or something?"

"No. Not that. Just think a minute. What if you haven't died yet? What if you're still alive?" As she said it, it all became clearer to Melissa. She knew she was right. She *had* to be right.

"You mean—"

"I mean you're a ghost from the future, Paul. You haven't died yet. You've come *back* in time, back to a time when you're still alive."

"It doesn't make any sense," he said, scowling. "I told you, you've totally lost it."

"Just think about it!" Melissa cried, too excited to get exasperated with him. "The Paul I saw at the dance club last night, the Paul with all his buddies— he was still alive. And the Paul who followed me at the supermarket parking lot this morning—that Paul is still alive. Don't you see? You've come back in time from the future. In this time—now—you're still alive, Paul. You're still alive!"

Without thinking, she ran over to him and happily threw her arms around his shoulders. She felt nothing, nothing but cold air.

Feeling foolish, she stepped back. He was looking hard at her, still thinking about what she had said.

"In other words," he said slowly, "you haven't killed me yet."

His words sent a chill down her back. She dropped on her knees onto her bed. "No," she said quietly, "I haven't killed you yet. That's why I had no memory of killing you. I haven't done it."

"But you're going to." He stared at her accusingly. "You're going to."

"No!" she cried. "No! Don't say that! I won't! I can't! I promise I won't!"

"I'm dead," he said glumly. "I'm dead and trapped in this limbo—and you did it."

"No!" Melissa cried, her voice choked with horror. The thought of killing Paul—of killing anyone—was too terrifying to think about. "No! Please, listen! Don't you see? This is a second chance, Paul. A second chance for both of us. I won't kill you. I won't! Just go away. Go away from this house—and stay away! If you're not here, there's no way I could kill you."

"I'm already a ghost," Paul said sadly. "It's the live Paul who has to stay away."

"Of course. Don't you see? That's why you've come back, Paul. You didn't come back to earth to kill me and avenge your death. You came back to earth to *prevent* your death! You can do it! You can stop yourself from getting killed!"

His smile was radiant, mixed with the sunlight streaming into the room, a clean, white light, so bright Melissa had to shield her eyes with her hand. When she lowered her hand, Paul was standing in front of her.

It was his turn to try to hug her. He leaned down. His arms went around her shoulders. "Can you . . . feel anything?" he asked.

"Yes," she answered truthfully. "It isn't cold. The air is warm now. I can almost feel you, Paul."

Still smiling, he stepped back. "I'm getting strong again. Thanks, Melissa."

"I didn't really do anything," she said uncomforta-

124

bly. She suddenly realized, to her surprise, that she cared about him, about what happened to him.

"Yeah, you did. You helped figure this all out. You helped me to have a second chance. And I'm not going to blow it. I'm not."

"I'll help," she said, thinking about how sweet and boyish he was once you got past the tough exterior, the bitterness in his eyes. "I'll take you to him. I'll take you to the live Paul, tonight! You've got to warn him. You've got to stop him from getting killed!"

chapter
17

Paul's house stood in a line of graying clapboard row houses in a run-down neighborhood west of the Old Village. A scrawny black cat scratched through a torn plastic garbage bag on the front stoop. A few stoops down the row, two teenage girls in jeans and black leather jackets were having a loud argument, ignoring a neighbor, who leaned out a ground-floor window, pleading desperately for them to shut up.

Melissa parked the car and locked it. She wondered if the car would be okay in this neighborhood.

At first, Paul didn't recognize the house. "This isn't it," he said. "It doesn't look right."

"But you said Frankie was your neighbor, right?" Melissa insisted. "Well, I looked up Frankie's address in the phone book. He lives at thirty-six. So your house must be thirty-four or thirty-eight."

Paul, his face as gray as the evening light, shook his head uncertainly and looked up at the dark, dirty windows of the houses. "Maybe," he said finally, his voice a whisper. "Maybe."

Two teenage boys, wearing only jeans and T-shirts despite the coolness of the evening, came running at full speed around the corner. Melissa had to leap to the side to get out of their way. They laughed and kept running without turning back.

To her surprise, Paul was already halfway up the steps to number thirty-four. "This is it," he said. "Yes. This is my house. There's my name on the mailbox. Starett. I can remember it now. All of a sudden, I have all these memories." He didn't seem happy about them, only overwhelmed, filled with sadness, filled with apprehension. "I'm going in," he said. "Come with me."

"I can't," she called up to him. "He'll see me."

He turned and looked down at her from the top of the stoop. "You're right. Okay. Wait for me. Wish me luck." He tried to make it sound light, but his wavering voice revealed how worried he was.

"Good luck," Melissa said, sitting down uncomfortably on a cold granite step. She watched him walk through the front door without opening it. If he succeeds, if he can communicate with the live Paul, he'll go away and I'll never see him again, she thought.

To her surprise, she wasn't sure how she felt about that.

* * *
127

The ghost Paul floated through his old living room, dark and empty. The furniture looked familiar even though a few seconds earlier he had no recollection of any of it. He stopped to rub his hand over the worn corduroy couch.

Without realizing it, he cried out. It was as if he were dying all over again, losing everything, losing this house, his friends, losing his memories, everything that mattered to him.

I can't go through with this, he thought. It's just too painful. I can't bear it.

He heard a noise in the back. The sound of shoes scraping against the floor. A cough.

He moved away from the old couch and headed toward the back. His bedroom was there, he suddenly remembered. He could picture it so clearly. The long, narrow room. The bunk bed against the wall. The folding chair in front of the low, white counter that served as his desk.

The door to his room was open. The light was on. He hesitated a few feet from the doorway. He could feel his energy level surge.

Without any further hesitation, he slid silently through the doorway and floated into the narrow room.

And saw—himself.

Sitting on the lower bunk, illuminated by the shadeless, red table lamp on the low counter, there he was. How strange to walk into a room and find yourself. How frightening.

How sad.

The ghost Paul drifted closer, into the center of the narrow room. The live Paul tilted a beer can up to his mouth until it was empty. Then he crushed the can in his hand and tossed it toward the small, black wastebasket across the room.

He was dressed identically to the ghost, his denim jacket open to reveal a yellow T-shirt underneath, his jeans faded and stained. He ran his hands back through his long, black hair and stood up somewhat shakily.

The ghost started to call to him, then stopped. Paul had walked to the kitchen and pulled the phone book out from the shelf under the counter. He opened it and began searching for a name, moving his finger slowly down the columns.

Then he picked up the phone, an uncertain look on his face. He pushed a number, referring back to the phone book twice as he pushed it. He leaned his elbow against the counter and waited.

"Hello. Is Melissa there?"

The ghost moved closer, realizing that Paul was calling Melissa.

"No. This is just a friend," Paul said, sounding disappointed. "My name? It doesn't matter." He hung up the receiver and kicked the counter angrily.

"It doesn't matter," he repeated bitterly to himself.

Paul kicked the counter again, then, looking out the window, started to button his jacket.

He's going out. I'd better materialize now, the ghost thought.

He stepped in front of Paul.

"Don't be afraid."

Paul finished buttoning his jacket, turned, and headed out the kitchen door.

"Can you hear me?" the ghost called, following behind him.

Paul quickly walked back to his room, picked up a hairbrush from the dresser top, and, tilting his head to the side, began brushing his dark hair straight back, staring at himself in the rectangular mirror above the dresser.

"Turn around!" the ghost yelled. "You've *got* to hear me. You've *got* to!"

Whistling to himself, Paul tilted his head the other way and continued to brush his hair.

Desperately, the ghost stepped forward and grabbed at the hairbrush. But his hand went right through it. Paul's quick brush strokes weren't interrupted.

"Please—turn around! Can't you hear me?"

There was no answer. Paul didn't see or hear him, or even sense a presence in the room.

The ghost concentrated his energy, tried harder to appear. Paul turned off the lamp and headed down the long hall, then out the front door.

Would he run into Melissa on the stoop? the ghost wondered. He floated through the front wall of the house. Paul was already down the steps and jogging toward Davis Street. Melissa was nowhere to be seen.

Paul entered Aldo's, the liquor store on the corner. A minute later he came out carrying a brown paper bag. Walking jauntily, he headed out to the parking lot at the side of the store. "Hey, Kenny, Frankie—what are you bozos doing here?"

His buddies, talking under the silver light of a low street lamp in front of the parking lot, interrupted their conversation and came hurrying up to him. "You got beer?" Frankie asked, grabbing at the brown paper bag.

"Not for you," Paul told him, swinging the bag out of his reach. "Beer makes you drool."

"So?"

"Where's your rich girlfriend?" Kenny, a skinny guy with a serious acne problem, asked Paul.

Paul flashed him a dirty look. "Who?"

"That rich girl with all the hair."

Frankie and Kenny both burst into high-pitched laughter and slapped each other a hard high five.

"You been giving her what she wants?" Kenny asked, leering.

Frankie made another unsuccessful grab for the beer.

"I can have her anytime I want," Paul bragged, tapping himself on the chest. His two friends laughed again.

"Then how come she came to see *me?*" Frankie asked, grinning. "This morning. At the supermarket."

"So *that's* why she was at the supermarket." Paul glared at Frankie suspiciously. "What'd she want?"

"My bod, I guess." Frankie and Kenny exchanged high fives again.

"Right," Paul said sarcastically. "What'd she want?"

"Give me a beer and I'll tell you," Frankie said.

"Me too," Kenny added quickly, reaching out his hand.

"Tell me, or you'll be eating the cans," Paul said menacingly.

The grins faded from their faces. It was obvious that they were afraid of him. "She came to ask me about you," Frankie admitted.

"What'd she want to know?" Paul demanded.

"Hey, you guys," a man's voice called from the street. "Get moving. Don't hang around here."

They looked up to see a policeman's head poking out of a black-and-white cruiser.

"We were just going, Officer," Paul said politely, hiding the bag containing the six-pack behind his jacket.

They piled into Kenny's old Chevy Malibu, parked at the edge of the lot. The ghost Paul followed, wondering how to reach the live Paul, how to give him a sign. But he sank deeper into despair, feeling that he was destined to fail.

"Where we going?" Paul asked, seated beside his ghost in the backseat.

"We can't go anywhere. We've got no money," Frankie said.

"Well, there are ways to get money," Paul said, grinning.

More memories came rushing back to the silent ghost at Paul's side, night memories, memories of fear, of the blood pumping at his temples, of scrambling through windows, of desperate, dark searches, of grabbing what should have been his.

"You really break into houses?" Frankie asked, turning around in the passenger seat to look at Paul.

Paul nodded, swallowing a mouthful of beer. "No big deal."

"All those houses on Fear Street?" Kenny asked, more than a little awe in his voice. "All those stories in the paper? They're really about you?"

"I said there are ways to get money," Paul said smugly.

"They're calling you the Fear Street Prowler," Kenny said. "You're famous!"

"I don't care about that," Paul replied quietly, staring out the window as the dark houses and trees whirred by.

Paul's words jarred more memories for his ghost. Yes. Of course. How could he have forgotten? He—Paul—was the Fear Street Prowler.

But now he had to stop Paul. He had to keep him away from Fear Street.

But how?

Everything went white. He was leaving, leaving them, leaving the car, drifting into the blank world where he spent so much of his time. Struggling to stay with his live self, the ghost faded, ceased to exist. When he returned, it was some time later. The car was parked by the side of a road.

Where were they? The ghost could see a tilted street sign up ahead. FEAR STREET. He floated over the lawn as Paul made his way around the side of the rambling old house, keeping against the wall, tight in the shadows. He was about to break into a house.

No, thought the ghost. No. I've got to stop this. These break-ins will lead to his death. To *my* death. But what can I do?

In the dark he saw a rake tilted against the house a few feet from where Paul stood. I'll lift the rake, he thought. I'll swing the rake. If I can frighten him, maybe he won't break into this house.

Since fading into the blank, white world, he felt stronger. Strong enough to lift the rake. He drifted toward it, summoned his energy, wrapped himself around the handle, and tugged.

Yes.

Yes, he was moving it.

Finally, he thought. Finally I can get through to Paul.

He pulled the rake away from the wall, raised it in the air, and—

Saw that he was too late. Paul had already lifted himself up to the window ledge and was slipping inside the dark house.

Too late. The Fear Street Prowler was about to strike again.

The ghost let the rake fall to the ground, suddenly feeling powerless and defeated. When the woman's screams shattered the silence of the night air, he didn't move.

A second scream. The sound of shattering glass. And Paul came barreling out of a window, rolling as he hit the ground, on his feet in seconds, and running along the hedge toward the street.

The woman's screams continued. "Help! Help me! Please, somebody—help me!"

The ghost watched Paul run to the car and pull the back door open. Then, as Paul dived into the backseat, the old Malibu roared away, its lights off, the back door still open.

The screaming stopped. Lights came on all over the house. The ghost didn't move. He floated there, somewhere between this world and another, his mind in turmoil, feeling so light, so invisible, so helpless— so lifeless.

"Where'd you go?" the ghost asked.

Melissa cried out. "You scared me!" She had just washed her hair and had a green bath towel wrapped turban-style around her head. She wore a pale blue cotton bathrobe over her pajamas.

"Sorry," the ghost said softly, staring out the bedroom window.

"I couldn't wait for you. It was too creepy there," Melissa said apologetically. She sat down on the edge of the bed, tucking her legs beneath her.

"It's where I grew up," he said bitterly.

"Please don't be angry," she said.

"I spent my whole life angry," the ghost said. The darkness from outside the window seemed to seep into him until he was all shadows. "Being poor can make you angry. It can make you do all kinds of things."

"Are you going to start putting me down again for being rich?" she asked wearily.

"No." The shadows darkened. His voice grew even softer, more distant. "I saw you that day at the mall. I saw you get angry at your friend for making fun of that girl, that girl who was poor. I know you're different." He stopped. The room was silent for a long while. "But what difference does it make?" he moaned.

"What happened after I left? Could he see you? Did you talk to him?"

"No," the ghost explained. "There was no way. I can't change anything. I'm going to be killed—again."

"No! I won't kill him! I won't kill *you!*" Melissa cried.

"You won't be able to help it," Paul said bitterly.

"Then *I'll* go talk to him," Melissa said impulsively, playing with the silver pendant around her neck.

"What? No. That's impossible!" Paul declared, shaking his head. "No! You'll get hurt—"

"I'll go tell him to stay away from Fear Street. I'm not invisible. He'll listen to me."

"Why should he listen to you?"

"I'll reason with him."

"Don't be stupid."

Melissa looked hurt. "I'm not being stupid. I'm trying to help. You couldn't get through to him. So who else is there to try? Only me. Think I want to go see him? No. No way."

"You-you're doing this for me?" The ghost suddenly sounded truly moved.

Melissa flushed and looked away. "Well, yes. But

I'm also doing it for me. I'm just so frightened that you may be right. I'm so frightened that I can't breathe! I don't want to kill anyone. I don't want your insane story to come true. If there's *anything* I can do to stop that from happening, I'll do it."

The ghost started to fade. Now he was just a dark wisp of smoke, a thin shadow against the bedroom wall. "Forget it. We can't change anything," he said sadly and then vanished completely.

chapter

18

"No, I can't tonight, Buddy. I was just on my way out the door."

It was the next night. Melissa was preparing to drive to Paul's. She adjusted the phone on her shoulder as she attempted to brush her hair, which had decided to pop up on both sides like two airplane wings.

"No, I really can't," she said, trying not to sound annoyed.

Why did Buddy have to sound so concerned about her every time they spoke? They couldn't have a normal conversation anymore. All he did was worry about her and ask questions to find out if she was back to normal, if she had stopped seeing ghosts.

It was all so annoying. Why couldn't he just *believe* her?

"Maybe we can go out tomorrow night," she said.

"Call me at Della's. I'll be staying there while my parents are in Las Vegas. I really have to go now." And she hung up the phone.

She stared at herself in the mirror. The two wings of hair had drooped a little, but they still wouldn't lie flat.

Maybe I *am* crazy, she thought. Driving off past the Old Village to that horrible neighborhood to see that creep. He's just going to tease me and say that I'm coming on to him again, and it's going to be very unpleasant.

But if he doesn't listen to me . . .

If he doesn't listen to me—is it possible that I really am going to kill him?

No. No way. No way I'm going to kill *anyone,* not Paul, not anyone.

No matter how many times she assured herself, there was still a lingering doubt in her mind. And the only way to get rid of that doubt was to talk to Paul.

Melissa parked the car in front of a fire hydrant, locked it, and climbed the steps up to Paul's front door. It was a cool, crisp night, almost cold, a preview of autumn nights to come. Somewhere down the block she could hear the steady thud of a basketball bouncing off the pavement and the excited shouts of a playground basketball game in progress.

She looked for a doorbell, but not finding one knocked loudly, louder than she had intended. "Steady, girl," she told herself, glancing nervously down the block. She pulled down the sleeves of the Shadyside High sweatshirt she was wearing over straight-legged jeans.

She knocked again.

And waited.

The house was dark.

He isn't home, she thought, both disappointed and relieved.

What would I say to him anyway? She had tried to rehearse in the car, but hadn't been able to come up with anything that didn't sound totally stupid.

She knocked again, then leaned over the side of the stoop to peer through the dust-smeared front window. No. No one coming.

With a loud sigh, she turned and walked down the concrete stairs. She had started to unlock her car when she heard laughter at the end of the block.

At first she ignored it. She started to slide behind the wheel when she heard it again. She thought she recognized Paul's laugh from that night at the dance club.

She climbed back out of the car. It was a short walk to the corner. Why not see if it's him?

Walking quickly along the cracked sidewalk, she came to a small liquor store on the corner, a neon sign in the window proclaiming Aldo's. A narrow parking lot stood at the far side of the store. Illuminated by a low street lamp, three boys were leaning against a red Malibu in the parking lot, laughing and drinking from brown paper bags.

They turned immediately when Melissa came into

view, and stopped laughing. The boy in the middle, sitting on the front bumper, was Paul.

She stopped at the edge of the parking lot. Paul stood up and a smile crossed his face. He recognized her. It was too late to go back to the car.

"Look who's here!" one of the other boys declared, putting his paper bag down on the front fender. Melissa recognized Frankie, the boy from the supermarket. She didn't know the third boy, the one with the bad skin.

"You following me?" Paul called to her, straightening his dark hair.

The other two boys laughed.

"No way, man. She came to see *me,*" Frankie said, punching Paul on the shoulder.

Paul swung around angrily and glared at Frankie. Frankie backed away. "Just kidding, man. Chill out, okay?"

Paul swayed unsteadily as he walked toward Melissa. She realized he must have had a lot to drink already.

"I—I wanted to talk to you," she said, staying on the sidewalk near the street lamp, not going any closer.

"She wants you, Paul," the other boy said.

"She wants what you've got, man," Frankie added.

The two boys laughed and banged their open hands on the car. Paul ignored them and kept walking slowly, unsteadily toward Melissa. He had an odd expression on his face, almost a challenging expression.

Melissa stood her ground, determined to say what she had to say, determined not to be frightened of him. He looked so much like his ghost, she thought, a crazy thought. He looked like his ghost, but without the tenderness in his eyes, without the boyishness.

"Hey," he said, stopping a few inches in front of her. The light from the street lamp reflected in his dark eyes and made him look pale, almost ghostlike. "You didn't answer my question. You following me?"

"I *told* you. I wanted to talk to you," Melissa said impatiently.

"Oh, I see." He smiled. His breath smelled of beer. He held up the can in the bag and offered it to her. "Want a slug?"

Melissa shook her head. "You look like you've had a few already tonight." Why did she say that? She was so nervous, she didn't know *what* she was saying.

"Who are you—my mother?" he snapped, tilting the can over his mouth. He finished the beer, then tossed the bag onto the pavement.

"Listen, Paul—"

"How'd you know where to find me?"

"Paul, if you'd just let me—"

"How'd you know my name? How'd you know where I was? What do you want anyway?" He smiled, more a smirk than a smile. "You don't have to answer me. You want to go somewhere quiet and have a talk?"

He grabbed her wrist.

The two boys back in the parking lot cheered.

He glanced back at them, tightening his grip on her wrist. "Let's lose those guys," he said, pulling her.

"No. Let go."

He didn't let go. "Hey, you came to see me, right?"

"Yes. I have something very important to— Stop. You're hurting me, Paul."

Her protest only made him laugh. "No pain, no gain," he muttered and laughed as if he had made a very clever joke.

"Please—let go."

"Come on." Still holding her wrist, he pulled her close to him. "You want to talk? We'll talk, Melissa. Just the two of us."

· He pulled her away from the parking lot, away from the streetlight, into the dark.

No, she thought. Where is he taking me? I can't let him. I've got to get away.

She pulled back, staring into his face, and froze with fear. He looked so angry, so out of control.

chapter
19

"I know where you live," he said suddenly.

"What?" Melissa wasn't sure she'd heard correctly.

"I found your house. On Fear Street."

"That's what I want to talk to you about," Melissa said.

"You found *my* house, right?" He was twisting her arm. She wasn't sure if he realized it or not. "So I found yours. That's fair, don't you think?"

Melissa gave a hard tug and pulled free.

"Hey—" He looked confused, disoriented.

Melissa realized it was the effects of the beer. They were standing in front of her car now. She began to feel a little safer, a little less frightened.

"I want you to leave me alone," she said.

He laughed. "That's why you came to see me?" He

put his hands in his jeans pocket, then took them out. He didn't seem to know what to do with them.

"Please, don't laugh at me. I'm very serious. I want you to leave me alone. Stay away from me. Stay away from my house. It's very important."

A car roared by, tires squealing. The radio blared through its windows at top volume.

Paul leaned toward her. "I don't get it."

"I really can't explain," she said. "I'm just warning you—"

"You're warning me?" he exploded. "Warning me? You come to my neighborhood? You follow me? You're warning me?"

"You don't understand. It's for your own good. Just stay away from Fear Street."

She knew she wasn't getting through to him. She knew all along that she was bound to sound stupid.

I just want to be away from here, she thought. I just want to melt away, disappear.

"Don't worry. I'll wipe my feet before I come to your street," Paul said bitterly, staring past her. His face turned angry. He called her an ugly name, then turned and started back toward the parking lot.

"Please listen to me," she called after him, feeling like a fool. But what could she have said? What else could she have told him? That his ghost had come to her? That his ghost was trying to keep him from getting killed?

For sure. That would really make the right impression on him.

He's so tanked up on beer, he probably won't even remember that I was here, she thought.

That idea didn't make her feel any better.

Suddenly feeling very tired, she climbed into the car and headed for home. Paul's ghost warned me that I wouldn't get through to him, she thought.

He was right.

The next evening Della called just before dinner. "Oh, hi, Della," Melissa said, trying to pull on a T-shirt and hold the phone at the same time. "I'll be over right after dinner. I'm all packed for the weekend. I have so much to tell you about. I've been dying to—"

"There's a slight hitch," Della interrupted. "I'm still at my cousin's. I got hung up here. I won't be able to get back to Shadyside till tomorrow."

"You mean—" Melissa couldn't hide her disappointment.

"Think you could stay home tonight and come tomorrow?" Della asked. "I'm really sorry."

"No problem," Melissa said. "But I don't think I'll tell my parents. They'll only worry."

"I'm really sorry," Della said. "But at least we'll have tomorrow night and Saturday night. You'll be okay, won't you?"

"Sure," Melissa told her. Besides, she thought, I won't be alone. Paul is here.

Della apologized a few more times. Then Melissa said good-bye and hurried down to dinner.

* * *

"I'm really worried about you," Mrs. Dryden said, plucking a red thread off Melissa's white top. Dinner was over, and her parents were just about to leave for the airport.

"Mother, I'll be fine. Really." Melissa sat down at the bottom of the stairs and watched her father struggle to close the suitcase. Pushing the side of it didn't seem to help. Finally, he sat on it and successfully managed to bring the zipper all the way around.

"Well, what with this Fear Street Prowler still around—"

"Do you have to bring that up?" Mr. Dryden snapped, wiping his forehead with a white handkerchief. "Melissa isn't even staying here. She'll be with Della. So why do you want to *make* her nervous?"

"I don't, Wes," Mrs. Dryden said, searching the front closet for something. "I just said I was worried. There was a story in the paper yesterday about that prowler. He broke into a house just down the block. And the woman was home and surprised him."

"I really don't see the point of discussing the Fear Street Prowler now," Mr. Dryden told his wife. He buckled another suitcase and turned to Melissa. "You *will* remember to lock both doors, right?"

"Right," Melissa said, rolling her eyes.

"When are you going to Della's? Are you packed?" her mother asked.

"Yes, I'm packed." That was the truth. "I'm going over there soon after you leave." That wasn't quite the truth.

"Well, we'll call you tomorrow," Mrs. Dryden said.

"Mother, I'm not ten years old, you know. I really can manage."

"Where are my golf clubs?" Mr. Dryden demanded, pushing his glasses up on his nose, spinning around to survey the room.

"Golf clubs?" Melissa's mother looked as if she'd never heard the words before. "Oh, dear. You *did* say something about golf clubs, didn't you."

Mr. Dryden slapped his forehead in an exaggerated manner, sending his glasses slipping down his nose again.

"Hey—I thought this was a serious convention," Melissa teased.

"It *is* serious," he said, heading to the den closet to get his clubs. "And I intend to get in some *serious* golf."

It took nearly half an hour to load everything into the car. Finally they drove off, after giving Melissa a few more warnings, reminding her she could call her aunt Kate if she had any problems, and telling her for the twelve hundredth time where they had written down the phone number of the hotel in Las Vegas where they'd be staying.

Melissa watched them back down the drive. Then, giving them a final wave as her father honked the horn, she closed the front door and locked it.

All alone now. Even Marta had left, gone to Cincinnati to see her brother for a few days.

All alone. Except for a ghost.

She felt jumpy, nervous, butterflies in her stomach.

How silly.

It was so quiet. That was the problem. It was much too quiet.

She walked into the den, searched through the stack of CDs, and put one on the player. Music flooded the room. Loud, pounding dance music. She danced across the floor by herself for a few seconds. She felt like dancing. Where was Buddy? They could go back to Red Heat and dance till they dropped. Then she wouldn't feel so nervous.

Red Heat made her think of Paul. Paul and his friends out in the parking lot.

The loud music was making her nervous. She danced over to the CD player and shut it off.

What should she do? Watch TV? Maybe there was a good movie on. She picked up the remote control, clicked on the TV, and started speeding around the dials.

"Hey—Tom Cruise and Paul Newman." She'd seen the movie at least twice, but she started watching it again. About half an hour later, she turned it off. There were too many commercials. Every time she started to get interested, they interrupted the film for five minutes.

Now what? She paced back and forth in the den. But that was only making her feel more nervous. This is crazy, she thought. I'm an intelligent person. I should be able to entertain myself for one evening without going nuts.

She got a Coke from the refrigerator in the kitchen,

then went up to her room to read in bed. She set the Coke down on the table beside the bed and started to get undressed. Then stopped.

"Hey, Paul—are you here?"

There was no reply.

She walked around the room, checking to see if there was a spot of cold air, a sign that the ghost was there.

"Paul?"

Where was he? Wasn't he at all interested in what she had told Paul, in what had happened the night before?

"Paul—are you here?"

Where did the ghost go when he wasn't there? Did he just fade into nothingness? Or was he always around, always watching her? Did he watch her undress? The idea was sort of exciting.

Maybe he's here, watching me now.

"Paul?"

She decided to close the window even though it was so hot. She pushed it down all the way and locked it. Outside, she saw that it was a clear night, hot and still. Nothing moved out there. Not a tree leaf. It was so still, it looked unreal.

Feeling strange, she took a long sip of the Coke. "I'll just go to sleep," she said aloud. She looked at the clock. It was eleven-thirty. Early, but she could probably fall asleep.

She got changed into her father's old pajama shirt and slid under the covers. The bed felt warm, too

150

warm. She kicked the covers down to the foot of the bed and turned out the lamp.

She closed her eyes, tried to relax. But it was too hot. With a loud sigh, she climbed out of bed, walked over to the window, unlocked it, and pulled it up halfway. There was no breeze at all, but at least it let a little air into the room.

Back in bed, the sheets were damp from her perspiration. She punched and prodded her pillow, trying to get it right.

I can't sleep in here, she decided.

She got up and, without turning on a light, padded across the carpeted hall to her parents' air-conditioned room. Yawning loudly, she pulled back the bedspread and climbed under the soft, cool sheet.

The bed felt big and safe. The room was dark and fragrant from her mother's perfume. She felt snug and safe as a little girl.

She drifted off into a dreamless sleep.

The noise woke her up. The digital clock on her father's bed table said 12:13. She sat up, confused at first, uncertain of where she was.

The noise again. A scrabbling outside, against the side of the house. Something moved behind the window curtains.

Melissa knew immediately what was happening.

Someone was trying to open her parents' bedroom window.

chapter
20

*T*he Fear Street Prowler!

Melissa dropped her feet to the floor but didn't stand up.

Was this really happening?

She heard the scrabbling sounds again, and a loud noise that she recognized as a ladder being banged against the clapboards.

It all seemed to be happening in slow motion. She looked at the clock: still 12:13. Time wasn't moving at all!

She suddenly felt as if her heart had stopped too. Frozen at 12:13. I've stopped breathing, she thought. I can't breathe. I can't move.

No. This isn't happening. I can't let this happen to me.

She forced herself to stand up. She took a deep breath. Then another.

"Paul?" she called to the ghost in a quavering voice. "Paul? Help me!"

No reply.

With a trembling hand, she reached over and turned on the lamp on the bed table. Maybe that would discourage him. Maybe the light would make him go away.

She stood there, frozen by the bed, watching the window.

Go away, go away, go away.

She saw an arm reach up from outside the window and push the window open. Then she saw the long, black hair. Then the denim jacket.

He stepped easily into the room, the curtains billowing behind him.

"Paul!"

He brushed off his jeans and scowled at her.

Was it the ghost? Or was it the live Paul?

"I told you," he said, staring into her eyes. "I told you I knew where you lived."

It was the live Paul.

"Get out of here, Paul," Melissa said. She hadn't moved from beside the bed. "Get out of my house!"

She realized she was only slightly relieved that it was Paul and not the Fear Street Prowler. Paul looked dangerous, as dangerous as any prowler.

And he looks so cold, Melissa thought. Cold and calm, not the least bit nervous about breaking into my house.

He stepped to the center of the room. His dark hair

fell over his forehead. "I told you," he repeated. "I told you I knew."

"Please, Paul—"

"I'm not good enough for you, huh?"

"Let's not talk about it now, okay?" She backed away from him until she was against the wall. "You've been drinking and—and I just want you to go."

"But I've come to show you how good I am." His mouth formed an ugly smile, a cold, menacing smile. "I'm good enough. Really. I'm real good."

"Paul, I'll call the police."

He snickered. "I'm too fast for the police."

"Go home, Paul. Go home and I won't tell anyone you did this."

I'm all alone here, she thought suddenly. I'm all alone in this house with him.

She had stood up to him—till now. She could feel the bravery wearing off, feel the terror taking over.

He could do anything, she thought, watching him come toward her.

She remembered her vow to the ghost: "I would never kill you. Never. Never. Never." But watching this smirking, cold-eyed Paul approach, the words seemed empty, false.

What if he tried to kill *her*?

Would she fight back? Would she defend herself?

No. No. No. This can't be happening. I can't kill him.

But what if . . .

"Come on, Melissa. No more teasing. No more games. Tonight's the night."

"No. Go away. I mean it. Just turn around and go back out the window."

"But I'm good enough for you, Melissa. You'll see. I'm real good." He spoke quietly, but his eyes revealed excitement, every word sounded a threat.

Suddenly a picture flashed into Melissa's mind.

The pistol. The little silver pistol.

It was right there in front of her, just a few feet away in her father's night table. Waiting. Waiting for her.

Waiting to protect her from Paul.

No. No. No way.

She wouldn't shoot it, of course. She would only use it to frighten him away.

She was so alone, so totally alone. Did she really have a choice?

Was she about to make the ghost's prediction come true?

I don't care, she thought, her emotions swirling, staring at Paul, reading the hatred in his eyes.

I don't care.

I have to protect myself.

I don't care. I don't care. I don't care.

No. No. I can't.

She stood frozen against the wall, at war with herself, watching him approach. Then, without even consciously making the decision, she dived forward and pulled open the slender drawer.

There it was. Waiting. Waiting for her.

The small pistol seemed to shine in the lamplight. She hesitated for only a second. Then she grabbed it. It felt cool in the palm of her hand.

Paul grinned at her from across the bed. She raised the pistol, and his grin slowly faded.

"Get out, Paul," she cried, her voice trembling. She held the little pistol with both hands to keep it steady. "Get out right now. I mean it."

"Whoa, babe." He raised his hands, as if in surrender.

"Out. Get out." She took a cautious step toward him, pointing the pistol at him, studying his face.

"Wow. Is that a real gun?" He was making fun of her.

"It's real," she said. "Please—just leave."

He stared into her eyes and slowly lowered his hands. He seemed to be thinking it over, deciding what to do.

"Go now and I won't tell anyone you did this," Melissa repeated. She gestured with the gun toward the door. "Go. Please. I'm begging you."

But he didn't leave the room. Instead he walked up to the queen-size bed and, with a quick, frightening motion, grabbed the bedspread and tugged it off the bed.

He let the bedspread drop to the floor and, stepping over it, ran his hand over the smooth, pale blue sheets.

"Paul, what do you think you're doing?"

He smiled at her, his hand still on the sheet. "Nice bed," he said. "So fancy. So clean."

"I'm warning you—"

"Come over here. Why don't you and me . . ." He patted the bed.

She uttered a low cry and ran to the door. She didn't have a plan. She just knew she had to get out of there.

He moved quickly and blocked the doorway. Melissa couldn't stop herself. She ran right into him.

"You're not going anywhere," he said, grabbing her by the shoulders and shoving her back. She stumbled, startled by the force of his push, but caught her balance against the foot of the bed.

She gestured with the pistol. "Out. Get out." Her voice revealed how terrified she was. He had blocked her path and shoved her. What else would he do?

He took a few slow, casual steps toward her. "Go ahead," he said, an odd smile on his face.

"What?"

"Go ahead. Use the gun. Shoot me."

Melissa kept it pointed at his chest. "Think I won't?"

He took a step toward her, then another. "Go ahead. Use the gun. Go ahead."

"Paul—no."

He came closer, and closer. He was laughing at her now, challenging her, daring her to shoot him.

"Come on, girl. Shoot me. Use the gun. Let's see you do it."

"No. Stop right there. I mean it, Paul."

But he kept coming, one step at a time.

Her hand tensed. The gun was pointed at his chest, just inches away from him.

All she had to do was pull the trigger.

But she knew she couldn't do it.

"No. No. No."

No way. She couldn't pull the trigger. She would never be able to pull the trigger.

She started to lower the gun.

"No. I can't use it."

"Then *I'll* use it!" Paul cried and swung his arm up fast, startling her. He grabbed at the pistol. She tried to pull her hand away, but was too slow. His hand missed the gun and slapped against hers.

The pistol dropped to the carpet.

They both stared down at it for a long second.

Then they both dived to the floor, scrambling frantically to reach it first.

chapter

21

"**O**w!"

Melissa's elbow hit the floor hard as she dived. The pain shot up her arm as she reached for the pistol.

I've got it! she thought.

But with an angry groan, Paul shoved her away. The gun fell out of her hand, and he picked it up.

Breathing hard, his face crimson, he stood above her, waving the pistol in front of him. "You rich snob! You're dead now!"

He kicked at her, but Melissa rolled away and climbed quickly to her feet.

They stared at each other, breathing noisily.

"What good is all your money now?" he cried.

Melissa took a step back, eyeing the door. "Put down the gun, Paul. Stop being so dramatic. You're not going to use it either."

His eyes flared. "Want to bet?" He called her a stream of names.

He could do it. He could shoot me.

The bedroom door seemed so far away. And he was standing between her and the door.

She held up her hands as if to say, Okay, I give up.

His finger tightened on the trigger.

He's going to shoot me, Melissa thought. I'm going to die now.

She closed her eyes.

When she opened them, the ghost was standing next to Paul.

She blinked, thinking she was seeing double at first.

Flickering in and out of view, the ghost stared first at her, then at Paul. "No! I can't let this happen!" the ghost cried.

Paul didn't react. Melissa realized he couldn't see the ghost. He kept the pistol aimed at her chest.

"I can't let him do this to you!" the ghost cried.

Melissa tried to scream, but no sound came out.

The ghost lunged forward and reached for the pistol in Paul's hand.

Melissa expected his hand to sail right through the pistol. But it didn't.

The live Paul cried out in surprise as the gun flew from his hand.

With one quick motion, the ghost pulled the pistol away and tossed it toward Melissa.

"Hey, what the—" Paul cried.

The gun sailed across the room.

Melissa had to jump up to catch it.

As her hands wrapped around it, the gun went off.

"No!" Her scream was as loud as the explosion of sound between her hands.

Paul groaned loudly and grabbed his chest. A dark red circle formed on the front of the denim jacket. "Oh, no," he groaned. "Not me . . ."

He dropped to his knees. Blood trickled down onto the white carpet. Holding his chest, he slumped face forward onto the rug. He didn't move.

"Paul—" Melissa let the gun fall to the floor.

The red puddle spread out from beneath Paul's body.

"Paul!" Melissa ran forward, bent down over him, turned him over.

"Paul!"

He was dead.

chapter

22

Melissa stepped back from the body. She looked down and saw that her bare feet were stained with blood.

"Oh, no. No—"

The ghost was right beside her, staring down at Paul's body.

"So that's how it happened," he said, his voice a soft, stunned whisper.

"But why? Why did you do it? Why did you sacrifice yourself?"

He didn't answer.

"Why did you knock the gun away, Paul? Why did you *let* me kill you?"

He stood so close to her, yet the air wasn't cold.

"I—I couldn't stand to see you killed," he said finally.

"What? But you knew I would kill Paul if you took the gun from him."

"Yes, I knew what would happen," he said, turning to look into her eyes. "But I couldn't let him kill you. I—I care about you too much."

"I care about you too," Melissa cried.

The ghost pulled her close and wrapped his arms around her. He pulled her face up to his and they kissed.

"I can feel you, Paul!" Melissa cried. "I really can. I can feel you now."

She reached for him, but he floated away from her, a sad smile on his face. He started to speak, but the words caught in his throat. "I-I'm going, Melissa. I think I can rest now. I've been so unhappy. Caught between two worlds. Not knowing why. Not knowing what happened to me. Thank God it's over."

"But, Paul—"

"I won't forget you. I won't ever forget you. Don't feel guilty for killing me. Don't ever feel guilty. You were the only one who ever cared about me. The only one . . ." The words faded as he did.

He was a shadow, then the outline of a shadow. And then he was gone.

She stood staring at the spot where he had stood. She could still feel his arms around her, still feel the warmth of his lips.

But she knew he was gone forever.

It took her a long time to realize that someone was pounding on the front door.

Who could it be this late?

She stepped around Paul's body and ran to the bedroom window. She pulled it open, stuck her head out, and looked below to the front porch.

"Buddy!"

He backed up to the edge of the porch and looked up at her, illuminated by the yellow porch light.

"Buddy, what are you doing here? How did you—"

"Lissa, are you okay?" he shouted up to her. "I went over to Della's, but you weren't there. I got worried, so I came here. When I got out of my car, I heard a loud noise—like a gunshot. I was so worried—"

"I-I'm okay," she called down. "I'm so glad to see you."

She ran down the stairs and pulled open the front door. "I'm so glad you're here," she repeated. "I need help."

She led him up to her parents' bedroom. He stopped short when he saw the body sprawled on the carpet. He grabbed her arm, his face filled with confusion. "Lissa, is that your ghost?"

"No," she said. "That's not him. The ghost is gone, Buddy. Gone for good. That's just some prowler."

"I'm so glad you're okay," he said, putting his arm around her. "Thank God it's over."

That's just what Paul said, Melissa thought.

She leaned against Buddy as they walked downstairs to phone the police.

About the Author

R. L. STINE is the author of more than a dozen mysteries and thrillers for Young Adult readers. He also writes funny novels and joke books.

In addition to his publishing work, he is Head Writer of the children's TV show "Eureeka's Castle." And he is Editorial Director of *Nickelodeon* magazine.

He lives in New York City with his wife, Jane, and son, Matt.

WATCH OUT FOR

FEAR STREET™

HALLOWEEN PARTY
Available as an Archway book

The Halloween party was well under way when the lights went out. That was to be expected at a spooky Halloween party on Fear Street. But when the lights came back on, there was a boy on the floor with a knife in his back.

Just a halloween prank? Maybe. Maybe not.

For Terry and Niki the trick-or-treating had turned to terror. To their horror, they realized that someone at the costume party was *dressed to kill!*